Night of the Wolf

D0767107

'He was beginning to feel that m
involved in the life and death of Nikos
Kakoyannis than a mad old man meeting an
untimely end.'

Chief Inspector David Adam's suspicions
were justified. This case was to draw him into
an investigation of the works of darkness, of
unholy ambition and the ruthless pursuit of
power.

It was to cost him more than his professional
interest and judgement. And as he closed in
on his prey, he himself became the object of
attack. . .

In memory of Dad, who loved 'supernatural' thrillers

Night of the Wolf

CHRISTOPHER BRYAN

A LION PAPERBACK

Copyright © 1983 Christopher Bryan

Published by
Lion Publishing
Icknield Way, Tring, Herts, England
ISBN 0 85648 446 6
Albatross Books
PO Box 320, Sutherland, NSW 2232, Australia
ISBN 0 86760 425 5

First edition 1983

Printed and bound in Great Britain by
Collins, Glasgow

Contents

Author's Note

For obvious reasons, some names and locations have been changed in this account. St Andrew's, Holborn Circus, was not the city church from which David Adam set out. Indeed, I owe an apology to my friend the Venerable George Timms, Archdeacon of Hackney, since it is his church I have borrowed (not to mention Jim, whose study I have turned into a bedroom). Nor was the Academy's location in relation to the Bayswater Road exactly as I have described it.

Anyone who reads to the end of this will gather that the Academy is still functioning. That, alas, is true. Those who recognize it, and share the writer's concerns, must remain vigilant.

Chapter One

Kakoyannis

In a shallow ditch beside a hedge on the Wilton Road a she-wolf crouched, pressing her body close to dry soil and grass that trembled with the roar of passing traffic. It was a warm, bright September afternoon and the trees had just begun to change their colours. If you looked towards Salisbury, the cathedral spire seemed almost to hang over the road, as it often does on clear days – strangely dominant as you begin the last mile towards the city, and somehow dwindling as you enter the outskirts, not to recover until (should you choose) you enter the Close and there encounter the great grey building truly dominant, floating on a green plain.

A blue sports car, badly driven, whined near the ditch and the wolf tensed. But she did not yet choose to move.

A tall, bearded figure stood at the north-east corner of the cathedral lawn and gazed. Nikos Kakoyannis was not gazing at the college, nor at the few late season tourists who were scattered about the grass and occasionally brushed past him. He had eyes only for the cathedral. Ancient black clothing and fierce, ascetic features made him a striking figure, though there was something disquieting about him too. Several folk looked curiously and a couple of small boys giggled. One man made almost to speak to him and then thought better of it. But Nikos Kakoyannis noticed none of these things. He continued to contemplate the cathedral.

The wolf was contemplating food and home. Not, of course, as you or I might contemplate – calculating the next possibility, asking the next question – can we be back before nightfall? Rather as a dream, a desire, an emotion – visions of crunching, of comfort and security, floated before her. Earlier that day, when the door of the cage that normally secured her had inadvertently been left ajar, other visions had led her to dream of glorious fields where fat, meaty creatures ran far enough for the joy of chase, and then gave themselves to her.

Such visions were, indeed, of an unknown world, for Sabrina (she knew her name) had been born and raised in captivity, and her keepers knew her to be tame enough, in all conscience; but they were visions of a world infinitely to be desired, for all that. So she had slipped her cage and left the fair, sidling unobserved through the quieter streets of Salisbury (or at worst mistaken for an unusually large dog) until she came to the green country. Which turned out to be hotter, dryer, duller and dustier than expected. Sabrina had never chased a sheep or a cow in her life and had little idea how to go about it. Meat usually came in joints, at about two o'clock – which was now long past. Meat. And bones. She panted. As abruptly as earlier visions had moved her to escape, the present moved her to return. It was time to go home.

Nikos Kakoyannis had also made his decision. In fact, he had made it months before and this day would see the culmination of watching and planning. He began to walk purposefully along the path that leads to the cathedral's north door. More tourists flapped and fluttered around him. 'What about a bit of tea, then?' 'I saw a nice looking place on the left, just as we come in.' 'Jimmy, come here!' But still Kakoyannis ignored them. For a lifetime he had trained himself to sense power and now, where none of these dolts could feel anything but their bellies, he was aware of that power, beating from the north door. He was aware, and he would command. He entered the cathedral.

Chief Inspector David Adam cradled the telephone in his left hand, and beckoned to the Constable for another cup of tea with his right.

'Well,' he said, 'I don't know. We're questioning everyone on the roads in and there's been no sighting yet. If she's not dangerous, it seems better not to raise too much alarm.'

The voice at the other end spoke briefly.

'But that's just the point,' said the Chief Inspector, 'her keeper says she won't harm a fly. Not unless she's frightened – then of course he can't be sure. What's that?'

The voice said something else.

'Yes, well, I suppose if she did pull down a sheep or something we'd know where to start looking. But it wouldn't make the farmers too pleased, would it?'

Something more came from the voice.

'Hmm, well,' – the Chief Inspector paused, nodding a silent 'thank you' to the constable who was filling his cup – 'I think for the time being you'll just have to carry on. And keep in touch.'

A few more words were exchanged and the receiver replaced. David Adam gazed aimiably round the Incident Room that had been set aside that very morning at Salisbury Police Station to deal with the Matter of an Escaped Wolf. Fair-haired, burly and pleasant, he gave the impression of a man content with those around him, and unlikely to be panicked by escaping animals or anything else.

'The fact is,' he observed to no one in particular, 'despite the nasty things people say about wolves, there's actually no proven case of a wolf in natural circumstances attacking a human.'

The constable gazed at him blankly.

'At least,' concluded the Chief Inspector, 'that's what Farley Mowat says.'

There was a pause.

'Excuse me sir, but who's Farley Mowat?' asked the Constable at last.

'A man who wrote a book about wolves,' replied the Chief Inspector. 'This tea,' he added mildly a few minutes later, 'is horrible.'

About one mile south of Salisbury Police Station, Sabrina, having crossed the fields, was working her way towards the city alongside the Lower Bemerton Road. The road was deserted and David Adam's luck was out. Just about the time he ended his telephone conversation, one of his search parties (three bored looking young men from the fair, equipped with nets and tranquillizing darts) was told to quit its vantage point by the George Herbert church and see if it wouldn't do better by going back to the Wilton Road, and working across the fields. Thirty seconds after the men left, a grey figure trotted across the road, scuttled quickly to the back of the old rectory, and so came to the river. To say that Sabrina had a plan would no doubt be anthropomorphism; but by whatever instinct she had, she was moving to something very like a plan. Something led her to choose the way where there was maximum cover as near to the city centre as possible. When the time came, she would have the shortest possible dash through the streets to the market square and so to those cages which now beckoned so entrancingly.

Inside the cathedral, coolness and tranquil grey-green light, pierced by the sweetness of treble and counter-tenor, exchanging the awful solemnities of the Nunc Dimittis,

'. . . a light to lighten the Gentiles,
And to be the glory of thy people Israel.'

The words broke through into Kakoyannis' consciousness – 'the glory of thy people' – and for a moment he stood still. The glory. Instinctively, his lips formed and breathed the word in his own tongue. *Doxa*. What was the *doxa*? Then a single voice – the spoken word sounding over the amplifiers with sombre power after the revelry of organ and choir – 'I believe in God. . .' and Kakoyannis moved on. God indeed! They all taught the same. The Greeks. The Latins. The Jews. Even that fiercer prophet of the East who rose to proclaim the Unity. What was Islam if not (Kakoyannis almost spat the word) submission? And what had submission ever achieved? A thousand exiles, a thousand griefs, from the tyrannies of Nebuchadnezzar to the tyrannies of Hitler. Even the Christos, he had submitted in his own way, and what had been his reward? Torn body and broken cry, *Ho theos mou, ho theos mou, eis ti egkatalipes me*? 'My God, my God, why have you forsaken me?' What had submission done for him?

Kakoyannis strode forward. Here in this cathedral was a power, not to submit to, but to control. Years of work and suffering had prepared him for this night. Ordained priest of the Orthodox Church, priesthood had never been enough for him, and he had long since apostacized. Even as he had prepared for priesthood, already the dream of power, the lost wisdom of Numenor had beckoned him. Power of life and death. He was sure it existed. Certain figures of the past – Sauron and Mithrandir, Solomon and Alexander, the Christos, Napoleon, Hitler – all for a while grasped part of it. And all bungled, failing in strategy, or lacking desire. It could be grasped whole, and that possession was Kakoyannis' dream.

The dream had led to a lifetime of quest: to secret ceremonies in Prague; to the search for an ointment that could only be procured in Istanbul; to dark rites in Paris and the sacrifice of a new-born child. It had led to endless research – to the Vatican, to the secret libraries of Mount Athos, to the Bodleian, to the British Museum, where his dark figure made one more strange visitor amongst the many eccentrics who haunt that place. Once he had even discovered a manuscript he needed, an eleventh-century book of magic, in the medieval library of this cathedral. He had studied it as a visiting scholar. The cathedral librarian, a grand and courteous old lady, had received him graciously. Her own chief passion had been the cathedral's copy of the Magna Carta, which she guarded as her own life, and she showed no awareness at all of that other curious document which reposed in one corner of her domain, sandwiched between volumes of little read and uncatalogued plainchant.

Now Nikos Kakoyannis had a plan. A plan for a ceremony that would bring him power. Certain words after certain rituals. A particular call with the right preparation. The essential details reposed in the greatest of all his treasures – a black notebook that had taken three years to find. He had at last wrested it from the hand of a dying man in a garret in Marseilles. The notebook itself was a copy, made ten years earlier, of a medieval document that had then perished by fire. The copyist himself had died soon after. The notebook had passed to other hands and to others, slim, battered, apparently unremarkable, fifty or so pages of neat Hebrew, set between plain boards. Those who held the book always died, some within weeks, none after more than months. Some died of malignant sickness. Two by violence. One, apparently, by accident. One of old age. But whatever its form, destruction seemed always to walk with those who

held the book, as if life itself could not long sustain the
presence of the terrible word that it contained. Ever since
the notebook had come to Kakoyannis two months before it
had not left his person. At this moment it lay in an inner
pocket, next to his heart. Under its tutelage he had made his
plan, and tonight he would perform the ceremony. This
cathedral, burning with seven centuries of the Christian mystery, and not far from that pillared circle where the ancient
stones remembered still older mysteries, this cathedral would
be the place.

It was turning to dusk. Sabrina sniffed cautiously, crouched
under the medieval bridge that carries Crane Street over the
river. There was still a great deal of traffic. She listened, ears
pricked. Cars were revving their engines in the car park, and
lights were beginning to gleam in Church House across the
river. After a while she lay down, and relaxed again into the
shadows. Her way lay across that road; but she could wait.
She could wait until the light failed.

Chapter Two

The Cathedral

Nikos Kakoyannis walked slowly along the North transept, mounted the steps, and continued by the North side of the choir. Purposefully but discreetly, he made his way to the Trinity Chapel which was, as he expected at this hour, deserted. He approached the side of the altar and then, first glancing round to make sure that he was indeed unobserved, slipped behind it and waited, crouching and still. It offended him to crouch thus, like an ordinary thief, but small things give way to great, and he must remain within the cathedral unobserved. Evensong was ending. The grace had been invoked; the final cry for peace had been sung. Now there was fumbling for coats and gloves, and the gentle murmur of English piety ready for its supper.

Gradually the murmur died in last 'Good-nights', and the echoing footsteps of authority and reverence in their turn preparing to go home. A portly verger glanced into the Trinity Chapel, and walked round to check the Dean's door. His footsteps died away. A door slammed. Silence. The grisaille windows to the East were almost dark; dim light gleamed in the rich colours of the West. And Nikos Kakoyannis was alone.

There were still plenty of cars on Crane Street and Sabrina still crouched beneath her bridge. Hunger was growing, but she was patient. And she had no wish to face the traffic. One of the Chief Inspector's search parties had actually crossed the bridge and peered over on its way home, but in the gathering gloom nothing could be seen. Perhaps someone should have gone down and looked; but they'd been out for hours and they were tired and hungry. Anyway, the creature was probably in Andover by now.

Kakoyannis walked down the North transept to the Dean's door – a narrow entrance in the North wall of the cathedral which, from outside, would already be plunged in cloaking shadow. The door was locked, but within minutes the clumsy antique mechanism had given way to his skilled probing. He shot back the bolts, and it was open. This was the difficult part of his plan. The ceremony needed equipment, more than he could have brought publicly into the cathedral without attracting attention. Now – out of the door. Swing it close. Across the lawn, avoiding the lights on the path, to a small grey mini-van, rented and parked earlier that day. Good. It was still secure. Open the back. Out with the first suitcase. Back to the Dean's door. Repeat the process. And a third time. At last he stood again inside the cathedral, and mopped his brow. Next, the sanctuary. It was now almost dark, but his eyes were sharp and used to dim places. Without difficulty he made the three journeys that took his suitcases from transept to sanctuary, and began to open them.

Several hours had passed, and Sabrina was still under the bridge. By now, local television newscasts of BBC and Southern had made her a minor celebrity. Somewhat contradictorily, a spokesman for the Police had exhorted folk on both channels to take every care, and at the same time endeavoured to assure them that there was no serious danger. The populace, for its part, felt obligingly thrilled and still, on the whole, pleasantly safe. Sabrina knew nothing of this. All she knew was that the streets seemed quiet. It was time to move.

Ten o'clock. Two small, foul-smelling black candles guttered dimly in coarse stands on the high altar, inches away from the great silver candlesticks that are normally lit to welcome the Presence. In front of the altar, the contents of the three suitcases were now revealed: three oblong strips of carpet, laid side by side across the sanctuary to form a single square, marked with ancient symbols of power. The circle and the pentangle dominated; in their midst, the Tetragrammaton (symbolizing, so practitioners of the black art claim, earth, air, fire and water); near that, secret names in Hebrew and four other tongues. At the circle's perimeter were votive lights, sufficient (with the light from the altar) to silhouette the figure of Nikos Kakoyannis who stood at the centre, rod in hand. For two hours he had been thus, motionless, demonstrating a power of mind over body that would have left most men a trembling heap. It was well said by one theologian that the disciplines of horror are ten times more severe than those needed to produce a saint. Already, hours before (eternities away, it seemed to him now) he had completed the rituals required to begin this summons: the reversals of that constantly renewed submission to the Presence which had marked the liturgies of this altar for centuries, and which must, for the ceremony, be turned back. There was little sensational in what he did. Sacrificed cockerels, ritual filth, the chalice of blood – these things had some power, no doubt, and he had used them in the past; but they were for beginners; they could not render the austere vision and control for which he now grasped. Simply, and with absolute concentration, he had gone through the four rites that had dominated the altar over the centuries – the two English revisions of the sixties and seventies, the great liturgy by

Cranmer that had ruled for three hundred years, and finally the Latin Mass that had held sway in preceding centuries.

In all these forms the Presence had encountered submission and, for certainty therefore, all of them should be reversed. Four times, therefore, Nikos Kakoyannis went backwards through the great rites, reversing their order and intention, until the perspiration stood upon his brow. Then the first part of the ceremony, with its own blasphemous confession. And now, the vigil. The chalice stood upon the altar. Before it was the place where the demon should appear; and before them both, the apostate priest, directing upon them the eyebeams of his mind, and every atom of his will: challenging the reversed Presence to wrestle; to the awful conjunction of bent Power with bent Power, in his own service.

Kakoyannis was aware of rustling. Something moving, something breathing, something stirring on the fringes of consciousness. He redoubled his concentration. Who knew what discarnate entities might ride the storm he was creating? He must concentrate only on the centre, the focus of power. His eyes burnt into the chalice. Faintly, faintly, faintly, it was beginning to glow. Something was answering. Slowly. Slowly. The more concentration. The more stillness. The utter direction. The air above the chalice was darkening. Faintly, steadily there emerged a countenance: almond eyes, gleaming in the faint light. It was That which he had willed to encounter. It was the face of the Beast. And now must be the time. Nikos Kakoyannis called. He called with a cry that had not been heard since the court of Solomon; words of power that uttered their command, and were what they commanded. And the Beast came, sweeping aside the chalice, which crashed against one of the great silver candlesticks and clattered to the ground. And in the coming of the Beast, Nikos Kakoyannis learnt that all discipline had been useless, all learning folly, and all strength of will in vain: that he too must submit. In so learning, he died.

Quite how, or why, the wolf got into the cathedral, no one ever discovered. In one sense the 'how' was clear enough, for the Dean's door was still open. But the precise sequence of events that brought her there will probably never be known. Certainly, it was not difficult to make conjectures. The streets of Salisbury are quiet by half-past nine on a Saturday night, but not utterly deserted, and it was easy to see how the creature, getting as far as Beach's corner and then being frightened by some noise from the direction of the Market Square, might have bolted through the High Street gate into the Close; how then voices or a car starting from the direction of the Precentor's house might have driven the animal further towards the silent pile of the cathedral; and how, finally, headlights emerging from the Theological College — or even mere seeking for security — might have led her, finding the Dean's door open, to plunge through it.

At any rate, by the time Sabrina jumped on to the High Altar, she was sufficiently confused, sufficiently frightened and sufficiently angry for a sweaty, bawling man to have been the last straw. She swept aside the irritating metal container that barred her way, and sprang.

The precious ornaments at Salisbury Cathedral are (since precious in the eyes of men as well as, one hopes, of God) linked directly to an alarm system in Salisbury police station; and so, within minutes of the chalice striking the high altar candlestick, that tremor had produced in the Close an assembly of police cars, police motorcycles, searchlights and sirens such as had not been seen since an aged canon had thoughtlessly moved a candlestick in the Trinity Chapel one evening some years before.

The inhabitants of the Close (particularly the students of the two colleges) thought it a fine piece of excitement, and even the Principal of the Theological College (locked in preparation for tomorrow's sermon) paused to wonder in a soft, West-Riding accent, 'what the devil was going on'. The police arrived in time to ruin the Dean's second cup of coffee and his evening.

The affair did not, actually, make much stir. A corpse and an escaped animal were certainly a confounded nuisance from the point of view of the police and the cathedral authorities, but from the point of view of the national press, since they coincided with a financial scandal and a threatened rail strike, they were small beer. Even for the local papers, by the time they came out, other things had grown in importance, and the cathedral excitement made scarcely a column – filled out in the *Journal* with a picture of the Dean, and, in the *Times* with a rather thin editorial on what the writer was pleased to call 'the growth of black magic practices'.

Yet that editorial, with its mildly sensational headline, did succeed in gaining the attention of at least one distinguished reader. Dr James Darrell, prominent scientist and researcher (amongst other things) into the art of biological warfare, noticed it folded in the pocket of a junior colleague who stood talking with friends in a corridor of the Ministry of Defence research centre, a few miles from Salisbury, where they all worked.

'Excuse me – may I see that?'

'Er – certainly, sir.' The younger man sounded surprised, and with cause, since Dr Darrell was not noted for his interest in popular journalism, nor, indeed, in anything that did not bear directly on his work. Slim, pale and precise, he handled the paper now as one who handles an unfamiliar specimen, scanning the article quickly, his lips pursed. With a curt 'Thank you' he returned it and left. The younger man looked at his friends, raised his eyebrows, and shrugged. The others laughed. And the episode was forgotten – by all,

that is, except James Darrell. That evening, driving towards
his home on the outskirts of Salisbury, he stopped at a
newsagent. When he returned to the car he held a copy of
the paper he had earlier borrowed and copies of all the other
papers he had been able to buy. He shut the car door but
did not immediately drive on. Instead, in failing light, he sat
and read avidly all that the press could tell him of the life
and death of Nikos Kakoyannis.

Subsequently there was an inquest, at which it emerged that
there would not even be (for those who enjoyed such things)
the pleasurable horror of contemplating that a wolf had killed
a man. Nikos Kakoyannis had died of a heart attack – the
result of immense strain, followed by sudden shock. Sabrina
had certainly leapt towards him, probably more in panic than
with hostile intent, and had gazed curiously upon him as he
lay. But upon his form she had laid not one claw. Even so,
she by no means came out of the affair scot-free. Superfi-
cially, her hurts were trivial – a slight cut on her left ear,
where possibly she had caught it on barbed wire. She had no
other injury. Yet within days of returning to her cage she
was ill. Then she was better. Then (the fair having meantime
moved to London) she was ill again. A vet was called, and
admitted herself baffled. With yet another move in prospect
for the fair the vet was, however, sure that a long journey
was inadvisable. There were negotiations. And when the fair
travelled north, Sabrina found herself convalescing amid the
luxuries of the London Zoo.

For those with a passion for neatness, one irritating detail
remained unexplained. When the sanctuary was put to rights,
the Spanish silver cross that normally dominates from a stand
behind the high altar was found lying on the ground. It was
difficult to see how Sabrina could have been responsible for
this, since she could hardly have moved the cross save by

knocking down the stand. And the stand was unmoved. So presumably Kakoyannis had moved the cross earlier in the evening – unwilling, no doubt, that his rites should be presided over by so clear a symbol of submission. The puzzle was this: the cross also was wired into the cathedral alarm system. A finger laid on it should have brought into action the same alarms as were eventually triggered by the jarred candlestick. Had there, then, been a fault in the system? Careful checks were made, but none could be discovered.

Tourists continued to walk the cathedral lawn. Those responsible for the cathedral continued, after their fashion, to proclaim the glory of the submission. And the black notebook, together with other curious and pitiful effects of Nikos Kakoyannis, passed into the safe-keeping of the Salisbury police, whilst routine enquiries should be made for his next of kin. These enquiries seemed unlikely to be fruitful.

Chapter Three

The Academy

'We know then,' said Reginald Danby, 'that the method exists. We have, ah, good reason to suppose that Nikos Kakoyannis found it. The question that remains is, can we gain access to his knowledge?'

'Precisely,' said James Darrell, and looked expectantly round the Boardroom table. The governing body of the Academy for Philosophical Studies was assembled at his request. The setting was elegant. A comfortable fire blazed and crackled beneath the handsome chimney piece. From beyond richly curtained windows, the hum of London traffic came only faintly. For nearly an hour Darrell had presented the result of his research to the Board and his colleagues had listened, at first with scepticism, then with growing interest. There were details (painfully traced) of Kakoyannis' career. There were fragmentary notes dating from a period in Kakoyannis' studies too early to be of direct use but late enough to indicate the direction in which he was moving. There were details of the final scene in the cathedral, pieced together from newspaper reports and discreetly questioned local gossip. Above all, there was the fact (elicited from a stolen police report) of that baffled enquiry regarding the alarm that failed.

All, claimed Darrell, pointed in one direction. And the expressions on the faces of his three fellow board-members suggested that they, at least, agreed with him. Only the attitude of the Chairman remained, as always, indecipherable.

Few who looked at the polite facade of the Academy's premises in a residential street near London's Bayswater Road, or read discreetly-worded advertising that appeared from time to time in tube trains and well-chosen journals ('enquiries into philosophy and science', 'explorations into the nature and meaning of economics'); few who heard of the Academy's generous fund-raising activities for educational projects both local and national; few even of those who, for a month or so, attended carefully monitored and immaculately presented lectures on 'Western Philosophy from the Middle Ages to Kant' or 'The Rise of the Neo-Platonic Vision', gently delivered by personable young men in tasteful surroundings – few perceived the real goal of the organization to which they paid their fees. *Scientia Potentia Est*. Knowledge is Power. That was the motto on the Academy's notepaper.

For many (perhaps most) of its students, such 'power' meant nothing more dangerous than a chance occasionally to appear cleverer than their fellows. For a few – a chosen group who showed special promise – there were (after precautions taken and tests applied) first hints, and then (if response to hints were appropriate) gradually the revelation of something deeper, involving an awareness of those areas of life where reason and number alone do not satisfy. Spirit. Wisdom. Transcendence. These were the words used at first. Loosely used. Then the focus sharpened. Forces. Mysterious forces running through history, seeming always to bring down what logic and human skill alone would devise. The Life Force. Powers. Powers of mind, spirit, and the world, lurking on the periphery of consciousness, and ignored by scientific intellect because it cannot deal with them – but ignored at peril. Powers. And, finally, the Power. An ancient Lord, whom the Academy's teachers would not name. Those who perceived that Power, and served, would be gods among men.

Despite care in selection, not all who were chosen for this vision could bear what they were shown. Some did not understand. Some tried to flee – and found flight harder than expected. Blackmail was not unknown, and those who would not be servants often became tools. Several had breakdowns. These, from the Academy's point of view, were failures. Modelling itself in this respect on what it perceived of nature, the Academy did not regard itself as concerned with failures. Tracks would be covered, of course. Excellent lawyers were retained, all of them specialists in the law of libel. Beyond that, failures were merely loss. The future lay with those who could succeed.

The five now gathered round the Boardroom table were all of them those who would succeed. Moreover, they knew precisely how the Power would, in their generation, make itself specially effective. Their places in bringing that about were marked. Britain. Weakened and uncertain. Battered by inflation. Bereft of imperial greatness. Bereft, above all, of commitment to any metaphysic that might sustain her through material reverse. Hesitating on the brink of extremes – yet still possessing enough of her ancient strength to make her formidable. She was ripe for taking and, if properly controlled, capable of carrying the Power's designs far beyond her own borders.

The five knew what was to be done. Their agents were ready. They waited for a sign – the key to a ceremony of power by which they should set in motion the next stage, inaugurating a New Order. And the death of Nikos Kakoyannis was, perhaps, that sign.

They made, by any standards, a strange assembly and

many who knew them separately would have been surprised to see them seated at one table. There was James Darrell, holder of honorary doctorates from a dozen universities, and considered by many to have made the last decade's major contribution to the art of biological warfare. No one could deny that Darrell had come far. His parents had been respectable members of the working class, able to encourage him in his ambitions (so far as they understood them) but hardly able to support him in society. The little boy from the grammar school had already outstripped their modest dreams. Perhaps (he reflected occasionally in moments of self-awareness) his original drive for success had been simply the need to compensate for small physique and humble beginnings. If so, then life's triumphs, of which he had gained not a few, had not met this need. He was compensating still.

Next to Darrell sat Reginald Danby, dignified and portly, Member of Parliament prominent on the right wing of his party, and well known for his espousal of reactionary causes. By contrast with Darrell, Danby had possessed from childhood many advantages of wealth and status. His father Albert Danby had been a business man and entrepreneur of the old school, who made his fortune, bought his title, and married well. But he had been a man who believed in focussing all on the main thrust. So he had determined from the beginning to lavish the whole power of his business as well as the prestige of his title upon Albert II, his elder son. For Reginald, the younger, there was money, of course, and the ample prestige of the Danby name. But he would inherit no part of the kingdom. So Reginald had grown to hate the power he could not have, and to seek by any means a power that should be his own, always shielding his lust beneath an affectation of courtesy acquired from his mother, whose consciousness of the duty owed to breeding forbade her ever to admit an awareness of anything unpleasant.

Next to Reginald Danby, elbows on the table, work-worn fingers scratching his ear, was the tough, stocky figure of Tom Wardle, engineer by trade and powerful in the unions, where skill in manoeuvre had made him influential with both left and moderate opinion. Tom Wardle had once, in his own way, truly believed in the party he served and the goal of democratic socialism. Even now he had moments of longing for the old days, for honest hopes and good companions, thrashing out policy and arguing dreams over pints of beer. Still the elegance of his surroundings made him uneasy, and he loathed the pretentions of men like Danby and Darrell.

Opposite Tom Wardle were the hard, handsome features of Irma Ashliman, Swiss-born professor of comparative literature in the University of Edgestow. She held, in her own field, as many distinctions as Darrell in his, though her journey to this place had perhaps been less straightforward. She too had once truly believed – in scholarship, in intelligence, in the work of her own mind. Somewhere, somehow, she had lost that hope. More sophisticated in her thinking than Danby or Wardle, less so than Darrell, of all of them she now probably believed least even in what the Academy stood for. Certain processes, for reasons that were not entirely clear, appeared to produce certain results. So long as that happened, she would continue to use them.

Finally there was the Chairman, silent and unmoving, seated at their head. Of him it is difficult to say anything, since little is known. He was old. Apparently he, like Kakoyannis, had once been a Christian priest, though of what communion, no one could now tell. He had been glimpsed in the shadows, so it seemed, at several moments of history – as imperial Russia dissolved into chaos, as the Third Reich rose to its uneasy glory, and again in the agonies of its collapse. Long before Darrell had even heard of Nikos Kakoyannis, the Chairman had known his works, watching his progress with detachment. Now he watched the deliberations of the Board. He said nothing. He contributed nothing. It was not even clear that he was listening. Yet no one ignored his presence, and all who spoke glanced in his direction.

'There are, I think, two stages,' James Darrell's voice was clipped. 'First, the Book of the Ritual. We know that Kakoyannis was looking for it. The fact that he undertook the ceremony suggests he found it. That book we must have.'

'Do we have any idea where it is?' asked Irma Ashliman.

'I think we've a very clear idea. There are notes in the police report,' (Darrell paused to refer to a file) 'mentioning a black notebook found in the Cathedral with Kakoyannis' body. And the description fits – such as they give. Clearly they didn't examine it properly, for which we may thank them. As far as I know, it's still in their hands.'

'Meaning somehow we have to get it from them,' said Wardle in blunt, north country tones that had stood his reputation for honesty and plain speaking in good stead through twenty years.

Darrell nodded. 'That's right. Meaning we get it from them.'

'Police can be bribed,' said Irma Ashliman.

'Don't be too sure,' said Wardle cautiously. 'Some can.'

'But surely you already have a man – the one who obtained the file? Can't he be made to perform again?'

'Risky to use him twice on the same job,' observed Wardle.

'Of course it's too risky,' said Darrell, 'and I certainly don't intend to let him get caught. He's too useful in other ways. But in any case there's no need for it. I can get the book myself.'

There was a pause, as the others weighed this possibility. It was Reginald Danby who broke the silence.

'And you are saying, Dr Darrell, that if we obtained the book along lines that you would devise, we should then, as the Board of this Academy, be in a position to perform the Ceremony of Power?'

'That's what I'm saying,' said Darrell. 'We could perform the ceremony.' (Why did Danby always insist on repeating what you'd been saying for the last hour, in tones that suggested that he was making a major contribution?)

'And yet,' said Irma Ashliman, and hesitated. The others looked at her. 'Shouldn't we still need to find the right place?' she said at last. 'A focus of power? As Kakoyannis did?'

'I don't think so.' Darrell had researched the matter carefully, and was fairly sure of his ground. 'You're right about the need for a focus of course. But there's more than one kind. Kakoyannis needed a major site because he worked alone. Nothing else would do. And that caused him a lot of problems. To start with, in this country it meant a site rotten with Christian superstition.'

'Not necessarily,' said Irma Ashliman.

'Well, all right. Not necessarily. But in general it's so. And Kakoyannis at any rate chose a Christian site, which meant that before he could even begin the ceremony, he had to perform an enormous act of reversal. That, I suspect, destroyed him. Then he had the problem of timing. Need for secrecy limited his choice of time. The night he selected was possible for the operation – but only just. Another disadvantage. Now compare our position.' Darrell leant forward, eager to press his point. 'We shan't be working alone. We shall be five, and one of us –' (his voice dropped slightly, and he glanced towards the Chairman) 'a Great One. That means that in ourselves we already are a focus of power. If we got the book,' (he spoke with regained confidence) 'we could use a centre that had only minor power. We could use our own centre – pure of superstition, and needing no reversals. And we could choose the perfect time.'

He sat back, and waited for the others to respond.

'What if we don't get the book?' asked Wardle. 'Suppose we can't manage it? Or it's the wrong one? Are there any other ways?'

Darrell placed his finger tips together, and considered. 'Well, yes, there are. Or, to be precise, there were. Records regarding their recent use are confused.'

'What ways?' asked Irma Ashliman.

'*There are ways to communicate. With Kakoyannis. But they would be very dangerous.*' The Chairman's words were abrupt, and his harsh tones cut through the interchange like a lash. The room was suddenly filled with an acute sense of the danger in him. Danby licked his lips. '*So,*' continued the Chairman, '*you had best begin with the book.*' He finished, and withdrew again into himself.

Silence. Then the fire, which had burnt low, suddenly flared and crackled. The group relaxed. The decision, it seemed, had been made. Darrell would try for the book.

Chapter Four

James Darrell's Initiative

Chief Inspector David Adam could not sleep. He contemplated his wife, blessed with a deep repose that tonight seemed maddenly far from him, then turned on his back and gazed at the ceiling, faintly distinguishable in the darkness. Something in him, somewhere, was troubled. Whilst he would have been the last to claim for himself any of those brilliant attributes that make fictional detectives so effective, he was in his own way gifted, and sometimes cursed, with a certain dogged inability to overlook loose ends that had cost more than one West Country law-breaker a period in gaol.

In this case, the loose ends that refused to be overlooked were (of course) the alarm that failed and (in addition) the missing police report. Here Darrell's agent had made something of a mistake. It would have been wise to have had the file photographed or copied. To have removed it was inevitably to rouse the attention of a man like David Adam. Naturally, he was not within a million miles of guessing the real purpose of Kakoyannis or of those to be subsequently involved in what he mentally called 'the cathedral affair'. It was simply that somewhere in the back of his mind he was beginning to feel there might be an affair: that more had been involved in the life and death of Nikos Kakoyannis than a mad old man meeting an untimely end. Had there been accomplices? If so, what were they really up to? Had the same accomplices stolen the report? And if so, why?

He had himself been summoned to the cathedral only after the discovery of Sabrina – the whereabouts of the wolf being at that time his chief concern. So he had arrived later than the others. Now he racked his memory to recall the scene. The general disarray. The corpse, in ugly sprawl. The wolf, docile enough, a fleck of blood gleaming in the cut in her left ear (at first he had thought the blood was Kakoyannis'). The battered suitcases. All that was clear enough. But was there something else that they had overlooked? Nothing that he could remember. Was he then simply getting the whole thing quite out of proportion? A little mechanical incompetence by the alarm company; a little clerical incompetence by the police (and certainly *that* was not impossible) and where was his so-called 'affair'? Imagination run riot!

Resolutely he turned on his side, shut his eyes, and tried to sleep.

Darrell had decided upon a frontal attack. Kakoyannis had, after all, been a scholar and so was he. Why should not one scholar take an interest in another? Certainly their fields of study were somewhat different but would the average man make much of that? How should children distinguish the metaphysic of Plato from that of Aristotle? So, with admirable coolness, he went boldly into Salisbury Police Station, declared his identity and his credentials, and claimed acquaintance with the deceased. Yes, it was a sad business – a brilliant mind gone awry. No, he had not known the man well, only met him and shared certain philosophical discussions. But of course, he felt an interest. Kakoyannis had, after all, been a colleague, albeit an eccentric one. Were there, by any chance, next of kin to whom assistance should be given? Apparently not? Ah – regrettable. Alone in the world then. That was how these things happened. Well, never mind. He was sure that the police had done everything possible. If, on subsequent enquiry, they felt that there was someone he could help, he trusted they would feel free to contact him.

He was polite, placatory, and remarkably convincing. He made as if to depart, and then paused as if something had occurred to him. Ah, yes – there was one thing he had intended to mention with regard to the dead man's belongings. A notebook.

'A notebook, sir?'

'Yes – just a small thing – rather old. Black. It contained some philosophical and theological speculations, mostly in Hebrew. I lent it to Kakoyannis at a conference we attended some months ago. Unfortunately I neglected to put my name in it. But it is mine and I'd rather like to get it back. Is there any chance of claiming it?'

The constable on duty looked at the register. 'Yes. There does seem to be a notebook, sir. Let me check.'

Examination revealed that there was indeed a notebook, answering to the description Dr Darrell gave. It contained, as Darrell had guessed, no name. He had risked this, sure that no one would be so foolish as to couple themselves, even in writing, with such a dolorous word as this book contained – and the risk paid dividends. His story held. There were no charges pending, and apparently no other claimants for anything that belonged to Nikos Kakoyannis. So, when the request to release Kakoyannis' notebook was passed to the Superintendent, he, for his part, could see no reason why it should not be granted. The authorization was signed and within a few hours James Darrell was summoned by telephone to collect that which he claimed. Of course, he would have to be responsible for it, and in the event of any dispute

. . . but Dr Darrell quite understood. He continued to be urbanity itself, signed the appropriate documents, and departed with the notebook under his arm.

Outside, the sun was shining and there was a light breeze. He glanced about him, paused briefly, then went to his car. His hands trembled slightly as he examined his prize and then placed it, as had Kakoyannis before him, in an inside pocket next to his heart. Within minutes he was driving smartly down the A35, in the direction of London. A faint smile played about his lips.

Chapter Five

The Frustrations of the Chief Inspector

The adventures of Sabrina, like much else in a policeman's life, required paper work. David Adam tackled it as he tackled most things, methodically and in due course. And it was almost by accident that he learnt whilst doing so that Nikos Kakoyannis, or rather his effects, had had a visitor. Intrigued, he telephoned the constable who had dealt with the matter. Certainly, when the circumstances were described, they sounded reasonable enough. And in any case, was it likely that a scientist of Darrell's reputation would be involved in something outside the law? Apart from anything else, at Darrell's level of operation, an archangel would have trouble getting the kind of security clearance that the authorities must require for him. The whole idea was absurd. He thanked his informant and replaced the receiver. It was, in any case, time to go home. His parents were coming to supper and he had promised Elizabeth he would try to be early.

He tidied the papers on his desk, got up and went to take

his coat from the hanger. Then he hesitated, and returned to the telephone.

'That's right. Darrell. D, A, double R, E, double L. Anything you can find.'

Something from the other end.

'Oh, no. There'll be nothing on him. That's certain. But I'd like what information's available, all the same. Where he's worked, appointments, interests. The lot. All right?'

The voice at the other end said something further.

'Good. As quick as you can, then.'

The routine wheels of enquiry turned and David received his report on the life and works of James Darrell. It told him nothing. Everything the man was connected with sounded impeccable. His career at grammar school had been academically excellent, crowned with an open scholarship to St Jude's, Oxford. He had acquitted himself well in national service, gaining a commission and particular credit as a marksman in the process. His subsequent career as an undergraduate had, indeed, been disappointing. For some reason his work in the Honours Schools had not been highly regarded, and he had finished with a Third. But then a brilliant research paper had led to immediate recognition and from that moment he had not looked back. His research post with the Ministry of Defence, involving work at the highest level of importance and secrecy, was only one among many distinctions.

Yet David's doubt persisted. It persisted throughout the day and into the evening. After his supper, finding the unblinking eyes of Pooh the cat fixed upon him, he inclined to discuss the matter with her but she looked wise and went to sleep. Splodger the dog, similarly approached, tried to eat his slipper. He sat in the armchair by the window, an unread book on his knee, and gazed into space.

At half-past nine Elizabeth came home, late from an eve-

ning meeting with school governors, every inch the Educational Welfare Officer. Later still when she was barefoot,
curled on a cushion and drinking the coffee he brought her,
she looked less like an Agent for Law Enforcement – but he
told her his problems anyway. She listened, fascinated. Then
she asked why he didn't pay Darrell a visit.

'A visit?' he said dubiously.

'Yes, couldn't you say you were enquiring about relatives
or something? Then at least you'd have seen him. You'd
have feelings about a person. All you've got at the moment
are feelings about a file.'

David nodded slowly. 'Yes,' he said doubtfully, 'I suppose
I could do that.'

Elizabeth grinned wickedly. The tone of his reply was a
familiar sign to her that her suggestion had not filled him
with enthusiasm – equally, that he suspected she might be
right. The fact was, he relished neither the prospect of asking
his Superintendent's permission (as would be necessary) to
bother an eminent citizen for what amounted to little more
than a hunch, nor the prospect of actually trying to match
wits with the no doubt brilliant Dr Darrell. Both situations
seemed to offer unparalleled opportunities for making a fool
of himself. On the other hand, his doubts remained, and
Elizabeth's suggestion the only way he could see of doing
anything about them. Hmm. It was irritating, to say the
least.

Gently, Elizabeth intimated that if Mr Plod the Policeman
cared to look around him, he would find more interesting
subjects for his attention than Dr James Darrell.

With that, at least, he could agree.

The next day, David went to see his Superintendent and
found to his surprise that the latter appeared to place more
value on his powers of detection, and even on his hunches,

than he did himself. Permission to make the call was given and that evening he made it.

It was a disaster.

James Darrell was irritated and surprised by the visit but remained completely in control. As regards his surprise, he left David in no doubt. On the contrary, he succeeded very well in conveying the enormous inconvenience to which thoughtless interruptions put him. In the conversation that followed, it soon became perfectly clear that, regarding the affair of Nikos Kakoyannis, there was nothing to be added to what he had already told the police. And, moreover, that the Chief Inspector had not a single coherent reason for supposing there was. David had faintly hoped he might cause embarrassment with a question about the conference at which the notebook was allegedly lent to Nikos Kakoyannis. In vain. Darrell without hesitation referred to a consultation on the relationship between science and philosophy, sponsored in the previous year by the Academy for Philosophical Studies, an educational charity in London. No doubt, he observed, the Academy would confirm Kakoyannis' attendance, if the police cared to enquire. David did not doubt it either.

Would Chief Inspector Adam care to see the volume? Darrell produced a small black notebook, identical in appearance with Kakoyannis' own. It was, of course, a substitute carefully prepared against an eventuality such as David's visit. It differed from the original only in that the meticulously written Hebrew notes that filled its pages, whilst similar in calligraphy and arrangement to those in the original, contained nothing more sinister than speculations by long dead scholars on the interpretation of Torah.

Would the Chief Inspector care to take the notebook with him? Determined now to leave nothing unchecked, David declared that in view of certain developments in the case he would take the book. Of course, it would be returned as soon as the police had completed their enquiries. He tried to sound magisterial and in command, but felt merely boorish – an oafish constable who had rudely questioned a good man's word. Dr Darrell continued to be all urbanity. Of course the police should have the notebook. Was there any other way in which they felt he could be of assistance? No? Then that being the case – he succeeded in indicating an enormous pile of work that an unheralded visit had interrupted – perhaps on this occasion the Chief Inspector would excuse him?

'We'll return the book to you as soon as possible, sir,' said David in the hall, 'and apart from that, I hope I shan't have to trouble you again.'

James Darrell looked his visitor in the eye. Then, surprisingly – 'None of us *has* to do anything, Chief Inspector. We do what we choose to do.'

David stared back and for a second natural hostility between the two men was obvious. 'Yes,' said David coldly, 'it was a manner of speaking.'

'Ah, a manner of speaking. That can be very deceptive, Chief Inspector. Especially self-deceptive.' David's mouth tightened. 'I'll see you get the book,' he said stiffly. 'Good night.'

Outside, it was raining. He scowled at the magnificent grey Citroën parked in Darrell's drive and turned up the collar of his jacket. He had no raincoat (it had been fine when he set out) and by the time he walked twenty-five yards to his own more modest car, he was well soaked. He had gained from his visit a black notebook that might or might not profit him and a bad temper. In one respect Elizabeth had been right. Instead of feelings about a file he now had feelings about a man. Bad feelings! He detested James Darrell. In those last few seconds he had felt like punching him on his smug, intelligent nose. And it all, in police terms, added up to nothing. He got in, slammed the car door against the downpour, started the engine and switched on the windscreen wipers. One of them waved about wildly. It was, needless to say, the one on the driver's side. Muttering imprecations, he lurched out once more into the rain and adjusted it.

Chapter Six

The Investigations of the Detective Sergeant

By the time David arrived at his desk the following morning he was willing to forget the whole affair. Clearly, he would only make a fool of himself by pursuing it. Nothing happened during the morning to change this feeling. He applied himself to various matters connected with petty theft and traffic violation and so passed the time. Shortly before one o'clock the results of a routine enquiry regarding Nikos Kakoyannis' attendance at the Conference on Science and Philosophy arrived from London with commendable speed. The Academy for Philosophical Studies confirmed Dr Darrell's story in every respect. Yes, there had been such a conference as Dr Darrell described in June of the previous year. Yes, Dr James Darrell and Dr Nikos Kakoyannis had both taken part in it. The Chief Inspector grunted, and went to lunch.

Several days passed, and the matter of Kakoyannis had almost passed from David's mind. Then one morning he was approached by Brown, the rather bright young Detective

Sergeant from CID who had originally checked Darrell for him. Brown seemed to be somewhat elevated.

'Could I have a word with you, sir?'

'Of course you can. Come in.'

They entered David's office.

'Sit down.' He indicated the chair and sat himself behind his desk.

'Well?'

'It's something I thought might interest you. You know you asked us to get what we could on James Darrell?'

'Yes?'

'Well, I decided to dig a bit deeper after the report we gave you and there are a couple of things I've come across that – do seem slightly odd.'

'What things?'

David's tone was not encouraging, but Brown proceeded manfully.

'Well, first, I'm wondering if there's something strange about Darrell's early career. He really didn't do at all well at Oxford. Lucky to get a Third, by all accounts. Then he got a research position with a chap called Loveland. Sir John Loveland. Maybe you've heard of him. He was reckoned one of the most brilliant men of his day. A biologist.'

'Loveland. Loveland. Yes. Perhaps I have. Didn't he die rather oddly?'

'Yes, he did. But let's take it in order. The first odd thing is that Loveland took on Darrell. He could have had his pick of brilliant young men but he took on someone with a rather poor record.'

'Maybe he just saw something in Darrell the others missed. It's possible.'

'Well, maybe he did. Anyway, Darrell joined him and they worked together for two years. Then, as you say, Sir John Loveland died in strange circumstances. To be precise, he committed suicide.'

David looked at him enquiringly.

'Well, the suicide was a mystery. Loveland seemed in every way a happy, contented man. No evidence of depression, debts, family troubles, anything. He'd gone up to London for his daughter's fourteenth birthday. They'd had a little party and he'd seemed perfectly happy. Then that night he wrote a note saying life was too much and took an overdose. Just like that. His daughter found him next morning. Of course there was an inquest and in one way it was straightforward enough. All the actual *facts* pointed to suicide and there didn't seemed to be anything that suggested otherwise. Except, as I've said, that no one could find a motive. And that's where Darrell came in.'

'Oh?'

'Darrell had been in Oxford on the night of the death. He was called to the inquest, apparently to give evidence about Loveland's state of mind. They were, presumably, trying to find that motive. But then, for some reason or other, both the Coroner and a lawyer for Loveland's family seem to have taken it into their heads to give Darrell quite a hard time. Asked a lot of very pointed questions about his relationship with Loveland. Wasn't it true that they'd quarrelled – and so on.'

'Well?'

'Well, the fact is Darrell stood up perfectly well. The questions didn't get anywhere and on balance, the inquest's conclusion had to be for a straightforward suicide. But I think there was a hint of suspicion in the air. And it attached to Darrell.'

'So?'

'Well, the obvious thing seemed to be to try and trace the Coroner and the lawyer and talk to them.'

'And did you?'

'No, I didn't. Because they're both dead. And what's more, they were both dead within three weeks of that inquest.'

'Good grief. Didn't anyone think that was rather strange?'

'No, they didn't. I suppose unless you happen to look at the thing from the point of view I'm taking, there's no reason to. There was nothing else to connect the deaths, either with each other, or with Darrell. The Coroner died of a heart attack at his home. The lawyer was killed in a motoring accident in Cornwall. His own fault, by all accounts.'

He paused. David picked up a pen, and started to doodle. 'Of course, it could just be coincidence.'

'Yes, it could. Except there's something else.'

'What's that?'

'Eighteen months after Loveland's death James Darrell produced what everybody, I gather, regards as a brilliant and original thesis. On techniques of biological warfare. Since when, he's never looked back. Being of a nasty and suspicious turn of mind, I immediately wondered if there might be any connection between Darrell's thesis and whatever Loveland was working on. In other words – did he pinch the boss's work?'

'And did he?'

'Well, how to find out? That's the problem. Now, apparently there was a second member of Darrell's research team. A man called Travers. He'd left the team to take up new work about six months before Loveland's death. But presumably he would have had some idea where Loveland was heading and how far Darrell's thesis connected with it. So, it seemed a good idea to try and get hold of him.'

He paused.

'And?'

'And he's dead too. What's more,' Brown paused again. Like the man in the Bible, he had saved the good wine until last and could hardly be blamed for savouring it, 'what's more, he died on a climbing holiday in Scotland – three weeks after the Loveland inquest.'

'Good grief!' The bombshell had its proper effect. 'Good grief! Surely someone must have noticed that?'

'Apparently not. It's the same story again, I suppose. There was no reason to connect the deaths, unless you looked at them from this angle. And no one did.'

'And where was Darrell while all this was going on?'

'Thousands of miles away. He left England two weeks after the inquest, and was in the United States until just before publishing his thesis. Whilst he was away the three men died. Within three weeks. His alibi is cast iron. Unless of course you think it's just a little too good.'

'Hmm. So, we've got three men, all dying within days of each other, all connected by having something to do with Loveland, or Loveland's death, and all connected by having something to do with James Darrell.'

'Yes. In fact, if Darrell was up to something funny, they were all possibly in a position to damage him.'

'Of course there might be some other party linking them. Someone else we haven't thought of. Have you considered any alternatives?'

'Well, I don't see who else could have been involved in the research end. Darrell and Travers were the only members of the team. And Travers hadn't been replaced. And on the family end, it was Darrell they questioned so hard. Not someone else. He is the only link, so far as I can see.'

'Yes. I see.' David got up from his chair, wandered across to the window, and gazed out. He was well aware how pleasant he found it to hear Brown placing all these question marks against the career of Dr Darrell. And that in itself made him cautious. Yet, with all reservations made, it did seem that Brown had a point. There was something here that should be looked at. He came back to his desk.

'I've got all the files, newspaper reports and so on together that I can and they'll be with you this afternoon,' said Brown.

'Maybe you can get something else from them. I don't think I can.'

'You've not done so badly!'

'Thank you sir. Of course, it doesn't help that it all happened twenty years ago. But I suppose we're better late than never.'

During the afternoon, the papers that Brown had assembled arrived and David read them. He made a couple of notes. Afterwards he went back and re-read the material that had been provided earlier. It was then that he noticed. In the list of organizations with which James Darrell was associated. 'The Academy for Philosophical Studies. Member: Board of Governors.' He whistled, then considered. Of course, it didn't prove anything. If Darrell were sufficiently interested in the Academy for Philosophical Studies to be a member of their Board, there was obviously no reason why he shouldn't be sufficiently interested to attend a conference they sponsored. On the other hand, his being in a position to influence them possibly made their endorsement of his story about Nikos Kakoyannis a shade less impressive? He wondered. Beside the typewritten entry Brown had scribbled additional notes in ball point. 'Educational Charity. Started 1947. Chief business – running evening classes, all highly intellectual. Also goes in for fund-raising for other people's educational schemes. Last year made a big contribution to the new Cranston College of Science (government sponsored – East London). Only thing against them – brush with Charity Commsnrs. in 1970 – use of funds – question of political involvement – put right – no action taken.'

David read it through twice, wrinkled his nose, and considered again. It hardly amounted to a criminal indictment. And yet. . . ? and yet. . . ? Slowly, he reached for the telephone.

'Geoff, do we know any more about the Academy for Philosophical Studies than we've got here?'

'Not at the moment we don't.'

'Well – there may be nothing in it – but, when you've a chance, keep sniffing, will you? I've a feeling about that place.'

'OK, chief,' said Brown irreverently, 'anything you say.'

'Right. Then there's a couple of other things we could follow up from the inquest.' David paused and referred to his notes. Outside his window the clouds had cleared. It looked like being a fine evening.

Chapter Seven

The Decision

David's visit to Darrell and the Metropolitan Police's subsequent enquiries had actually caused more confusion at the Academy than David knew. Darrell had been genuinely surprized that someone was still interested in Kakoyannis' death, and though the substitute notebook had already been prepared, only hurried phone calls to London and an even more hurried adjustment of the Academy's records had enabled them to give the appropriate information of Darrell's story.

The next board meeting began with routine business. Irma Ashliman reported on a major project – the Academy's link with the new Cranston College of Science and Technology. To be sited in the heart of what had once been London's dockland, Cranston was an important factor in long-term government plans to increase the availability of scientific training at university level throughout Britain. Occupying a wide area on the north bank of the River Thames below Tower Hamlets and above Limehouse, it would, when fully operational, offer over four hundred places for studies in engineering, applied science, sociology, behavioural psychology, management and related subjects. The facilities available would be the most up-to-date and extensive in the country – in some respects, in the world. The project was financed mainly by government; but a condition of this finance had been the additional provision of considerable funds from voluntary sources and it was here that the Academy for Philosophical Studies had become involved. The Academy had been able to offer an astonishingly large sum from its own funds and in the straitened economic circumstances of the period this offer had been accepted with alacrity. In return, the Academy's nominees would receive a share in formulating the policies and design of the project.

'I am happy to tell you,' said Irma Ashliman, 'that building is on schedule, and there is every prospect that the plant will be complete in time for the intake of students in October next year. Our own influence on the thinking of the institution grows daily, and will amply repay, I believe, our participation in the financial investment. Should the position of this Academy be in any way jeopardized in the future,' (here she looked pointedly at Darrell) 'I believe it would be possible, in time, for our entire operation to be transferred there. In any event, both before and after the establishment of the New Order, it appears to me that Cranston College can provide, as we hoped, a valuable recruiting office where we shall be able to work amongst the best young scientific brains available. Whilst none of us would wish to underrate the value of this Academy as a recruiting centre, we cannot deny that our clientele in general tend to certain obvious limitations of character and intellect. The enrolment of Cranston College will be altogether wider and more satisfactory in scope.

'There is also another matter to be considered.' She paused and looked at the Chairman, who made no reaction whatever. Apparently she found that sufficient encouragement to go on. 'It is becoming evident that, as we suspected, the area to be occupied by Cranston does contain an ancient and valuable centre of power – the site known, at least since the sixteenth century, as Hadrian's Grave. Of course, it has nothing to do with Hadrian. We can now state positively that it was used as a base for the mysteries of the Mithras superstition as early as the third century. According to several authorities, it vastly exceeds the potentiality of anything we have yet controlled, being entirely free of Christian influence, and already affected by a powerful act of reversal at some time in the more recent past – possibly the eighteenth century. Naturally, we must proceed cautiously.

'We have managed to persuade the governors of Cranston that the site is structurally dangerous, and would cost an enormous sum to make safe. At the same time we have pointed out that it is, potentially, of historic interest and that there might be a public outcry if it were damaged. We have suggested, therefore, that it be sealed off, and we have offered the services of experts whom we will provide to supervise this, and, in time, to oversee proper examination. The governors have accepted our offer eagerly. The last thing they want to be bothered with at present is fuss about a historic site and our offer enables them to feel that they have acted responsibly, whilst putting them to minimum trouble. We therefore have virtual control, including control of access. Our researches and restoration are proceeding.'

She shuffled her papers together and sat down, amidst murmurs of approval.

The final matter on the agenda had been introduced by Irma Ashliman and Tom Wardle jointly, as a matter of emergency. It concerned police enquiries at the Academy and Darrell's part in allowing them to happen. The style of routine formality which had dominated the earlier part of the proceedings disappeared. Irma Ashliman was plainly angry.

'You must,' she declared, 'have been out of your mind. Do you realize what you did? Not merely drew attention to yourself, which is dangerous enough, you drew attention to the Academy. Are you mad?'

'Too clever by half,' said Tom Wardle.

'At least, at the very least, why didn't you warn us before-hand? I do not appreciate urgent phone calls bringing me here at eleven o'clock at night to correct your foolishness.'

The Chairman stared stonily into space.

Darrell was put out. He was also aware that failure in this affair could endanger his position. But he remained convinced that his colleagues were mistaken in their estimate of what was happening.

Of course (he observed) he respected their concern. And regretted the disturbance that had been caused. But he was quite certain that there was no ground at all for serious alarm. It was, to begin with, perfectly clear that the police officer who called at his home knew nothing. Absolutely nothing. He had been acting on a hunch.

'And what, do you think, caused that?' demanded Irma Ashliman.

'If anything, it was probably the file,' replied Darrell promptly.

'The file?'

'Yes. The police file. We needed the information in it but we should have had it copied. To remove it was an error — for which I take full responsibility. And in my view it's the only thing that has made the police look twice at this matter.'

'And now that they have?'

'Now that they have, what good will it do them? What in fact is there for them to discover?'

'Plenty!' muttered Tom Wardle.

'Of course,' said Darrell,' but not in this matter. We must remember what the police actually think they are investigating. The death of Nikos Kakoyannis. We didn't cause that death. We knew nothing of it. There's nothing for them to learn.'

'Rubbish,' said Wardle. 'You've lied to the police yourself. You've given them a forged document. And you've forced us to lie. What if they find that out? It's not bad for starters, is it?'

'And you know as well as we do,' said Irma Ashliman, 'that if the police once really become interested in this Academy, there is a great deal for them to discover. It is only a question of time.'

'Exactly!' said Darrell. 'Time. And time is the one thing they haven't got. Consider the position. Of course I've taken a risk. And of course the police could get closer to us – eventually. But for the present they have no idea what they're looking for and if the enquiry here didn't satisfy them, they'll be running routine checks. On the Academy. On me. On you. All of which will produce very little – to start with. A question here. A coincidence there. And whilst they spend time on that – we already have the book. And in only three days it is October the thirty-first, All Hallows Eve. The supreme night for the Ceremony of Power. We can do it! And once we have, it won't matter two pins what the police discover.'

He stopped.

'Three days. It's still damned dangerous,' muttered Wardle.

'Of course it's dangerous,' retorted Darrell. 'And so is what we're about. Whoever achieved anything without taking risks?'

The Chairman coughed.

In an instant attention was focussed upon him. 'All Hallows Eve. It is fitting.' He paused. 'The police,' he looked at Darrell, 'suspect something of you, but nothing to the purpose. They also,' he looked into space once more, 'suspect the Academy, but of what they do not know. You are correct. In three days they will do little. It is satisfactory. Arrange the ceremony. And inform the agents.'

He rose, and creaked slowly from the room.

Again there was silence, and Darrell began gathering together his papers. Reginald Danby had refrained from taking part in the criticism, suspecting which way the wind might blow. This seemed to him a moment to capitalize upon that situation.

'If I may venture an opinion, ah, lady and gentleman, it seems to me that we owe a considerable debt to the initiative of our esteemed colleague, Dr Darrell. I should like to place on record. . .'

But Tom Wardle had had enough. It was irritating that Darrell should again (apparently) be right. Now to endure Danby's cant was too much. 'Come off it, Danby. You thought he was up the pole as much as any of us. The only difference between you and us for the last twenty minutes was you had enough bloody sense to keep your mouth shut.'

'Mr Wardle, I must remind you – there is a lady present.'

'Oh yes!' said Wardle sarcastically. 'Some lady! Look – she'll be here on t' thirty-first for t' same reason as the rest of us. What she can get. Muck and brass.'

Irma Ashliman slid a cigarette into her holder and lit it. She had spoken her mind to Darrell and as far as she was concerned that was an end of it. Tom Wardle's outburst troubled her not at all. In fact, she was rather amused by it. James Darrell finished arranging his brief-case, then sat back and looked at Wardle with a faint, quizzical smile. He said nothing, but he was thinking hard.

Danby's wealth and the prestige of his name had made his support worth having in the past. On the other hand, with the coming of the New Order, these assets would be comparatively worthless, and Darrell rated the man's abilities in other directions at about the level of a chimpanzee. Tom Wardle was different. Rough. Crude. Overly direct. But concerning his intelligence and ability there could be no doubt. His support under the New Order could be invaluable. In the past Darrell had ignored him, having other fish to fry. The time might be coming to change that. Of course, he could do nothing at the moment – save perhaps sow seeds that might be watered later.

Danby was blustering on. 'One is of course aware that the development of the New Order will require certain individuals taking to themselves certain burdens of office. Members of this board will naturally be qualified in that direction. But one envisages only the highest sense of public duty. . .'

'You make me sick,' said Wardle.

'On the whole,' said Darrell, 'I agree with you, Tom.'

Both men stopped. Irma Ashliman coughed appreciatively.

'What?' said Wardle.

'I said, on the whole I agree with you. It's nonsense to talk about high motives and burdens of office. We're all here because we want power. I want it. You want it. Even the Chairman wants it – more than he has. And to get it, we need each other.'

'But. Look here –' began Danby.

'I don't like you, Darrell,' said Wardle, not at all mollified, 'and you'll not win me over by smooth talk. So don't try.'

'I'm perfectly well aware you don't like me,' replied Darrell, precise as ever. 'In general, I regard that as an advantage. Affection is a muddy affair that clouds the true basis of relationship. In our case, the basis of relationship is quite clear. We want control. As you said. But control begins with control of ourselves.'

Wardle flared instantly, as Darrell knew he would. 'When I want your advice, I'll damn well ask for it.'

'Precisely,' said Darrell, rising to his feet. 'And that may just possibly be sooner than you think.'

'To hear you, one might think you were after the boss's job,' observed Irma Ashliman softly.

'Not at all,' replied Darrell smoothly. 'I have as much loyalty to the Chairman as anyone here. The facts remain.

Until now, we have been playing at power. Soon, we shall have it. And when we do, we need to know what to do with it. That means, as Tom says, knowing why we want it. It also means knowing who our friends are, and who are our enemies.' He looked straight at Wardle. 'Think about it, Tom. Think about it.' He snapped shut his brief-case. 'I must go. No doubt I shall see you all on the thirty-first.'

He nodded briefly to each and left. Danby was speechless. Irma Ashliman grinned and smoked her cigarette. Wardle felt depressed. Darrell seemed to have robbed him even of the fruits of anger.

'Hello, what's this?' asked the rather striking young woman in a white coat who was about to examine Sabrina.

'It's the new lock. They're trying it out. You just press the red button.'

The young woman obligingly did so. There was a sharp, electronic buzz, and nothing else appeared to happen.

'Well?' she asked.

'That's it,' said her companion. 'It's unlocked. You open it and go in. Another victory for science!'

'Is it?' said the young woman. 'Well, I'm not sure I like it. That button's a bit easy to overlook, if you ask me.'

'O come on! It's progress!'

They turned their attention to the patient. The young woman peered down Sabrina's throat, looked at the injured ear, and carried out routine tests, murmuring as she did so endearments that Sabrina appeared to enjoy.

'She looks in pretty good shape to me,' she said at last, looking to her colleague for confirmation.

'Seems fine,' said the other. 'Shall we say another week to be on the safe side?'

'Right. A week then. Let's look at the others.'

Sabrina yawned. The two went on their way.

'Inform the agents.' Only minutes after the board meeting had ended, telegrams and telephone calls were on their way. Their message was cryptic – a single word and a date. But those who received, understood, and would be standing by their telephones on the night of the ceremony. There were forty in all; each member of the board, other than the Chairman, being responsible for ten – scattered in key places throughout government, industry, finance and the media. Each in turn was responsible for ten more – secondary cells, unaware of each others' existence and quite unaware of their part in an overall plan.

Immediately following the Ceremony of Power, the codeword would be given and certain actions initiated. Their effect had been calculated. A scenario prepared. Within thirty-six hours – a series of crippling strikes, affecting transport, power and food. For the next twenty-four hours – an unprecedented run on sterling, culminating in the collapse of a major bank. Then mounting frustration, exploding into violence. London, Glasgow, Birmingham and Liverpool had been selected. There would follow conflicting and impossible demands from groups on left and right. Finally, the well-orchestrated call for firm action. When that call came, there were those standing by who would be ready to respond. In them, the New Order would be born.

Chapter Eight

Questions from London

On the same day that the Board of the Academy met, David Adam went to London. He was required to present himself as witness in a trial at the Central Criminal Court, beginning the following day.

He expected to be three nights in the capital and, as always, had arranged to stay with his friend Michael Aarons. Traffic was heavy and driving in London as frustrating as ever. Yet that could not prevent the familiar glow of pleasure as he pulled his car to the left of the traffic in St Andrew Street and then sharply left again to face the green double gates that led to the vicarage garden. He got out to open them and scarcely had the second in place before a welcoming figure, grey-haired but still slim and dapper, was coming down the vicarage steps.

David and Elizabeth Adam's friendship with Michael Aarons dated from a time when Aarons had been Vicar of St Mark's, Salisbury. They had been among the younger members of his congregation. Later, Aarons had married them. Their relationship with him was a gentle affair, with something in it of father and children, and something of older and younger brothers and sister. A superficial observer might have found it strange that there should be anything in common between the scholarly cleric, whose delightful accent still betrayed his origin in the Jewish community of pre-war Vienna, and the young policeman and his wife, both Wiltshire born and raised, and English of the English. Yet something rich they undoubtedly gave to each other, and growing respect had, over the years, served to deepen original affection. When Aarons moved from Salisbury to take up his new work as Guild Vicar of St Andrew's, Holborn Circus, and Archdeacon of East London, it was natural that the Adams, sometimes singly and sometimes as a family, continued to visit him when opportunity arose.

That evening after dinner David produced the black notebook, and Aarons promised to look at it the following day. Then talk turned to family and friends, to dogs and cats (Aarons had two – a disreputable tabby called Albert who had appeared one day on the doorstep and refused to go, and Marlene, an incredibly beautiful Persian, who knew it). Old memories were recalled, and the latest stories exchanged. The works of Darrell and his acquaintances seemed far away.

On the following day, as soon as the Court was adjourned, David walked back across Holborn Viaduct to the vicarage and telephoned the station at Salisbury. No, the industrious Detective Sergeant Brown had not yet come up with anything that should seriously call in question the Academy's virtue. But a different line of approach had proved more interesting. At David's suggestion he had made enquiry concerning others who had been involved in the inquest. One was Loveland's daughter, who might, David thought, have some explanation to offer about the lawyer's hostility to Darrell. Another was the doctor who had originally been called to the scene of Loveland's death. The daughter, it transpired, was now working for the Episcopal Church in Alaska. After some effort Brown had actually managed to speak to her by telephone at her home in Anchorage. As regards the inquest, she was unable to help. She remembered the lawyer's strange manner but had not known what he was about. His death soon afterwards had prevented her learning. She had, she reminded Brown, been very young at the time. Then, without realizing it, she revealed a fact that was far more significant to her questioner than it was to her. Daddy had visited London earlier that week – only four days before his death. He had come to deliver a lecture. The lecture had been sponsored by an educational charity. For some reason she remembered the name. It was the Academy for Philosophical Studies.

There was a pause and Geoff Brown savoured down the phone his superior's sharp intake of breath. 'Yes,' he said cheerfully, 'I thought that was one more for the book, too.'

The doctor had been (from their point of view) a disappointment. He was a respected family practitioner who had been called because the daughter naturally telephoned the only doctor she knew. He had retired from practice three years after Loveland's death and lived another fourteen years in retirement. He had died at last in the country, surrounded by his family and of ripe age. There really did not seem to be anything to pursue there. David agreed.

True to form, Geoff Brown had saved the best until last. David had initiated an enquiry with his opposite number at Paddington Police Station regarding the careers and present whereabouts of two police officers, a sergeant and a constable, who had been called to the Loveland house by the doctor and had subsequently given evidence at the inquest. The results of the enquiry were now available. Brown read them in a voice that seemed deliberately expressionless. According to records, the senior of the two officers had died, four months after the inquest, of leukemia. The junior had resigned from the force a few weeks after that and all trace of him had been lost.

'Blimey,' said David.

'Yes,' said Brown, 'that's what I thought.'

They considered the situation.

There was still, of course, nothing tangible to go on. No demonstrable reason to connect Darrell with any of it. Yet they now knew of five people who had been involved in Darrell's life at the time of Loveland's death – five people who might possibly have been a threat to him. Of these five, four had died and one had vanished, all within five months of each other, and all whilst James Darrell was conveniently out of reach. It was incredible. Yes – that was it. Despite the lack of clear evidence against Darrell, the facts regarding that part of his life, arranged as they could now arrange them, were simply incredible, unless there were malicious design in them. And whose design, but Darrell's? And what of the Academy for Philosophical Studies? Didn't this new appearance on the edge of the affair just stretch coincidence a shade too far? Were they involved as a group? Or was Darrell using them? At any rate, there was much here that must be followed up.

They discussed next steps for a few minutes, chatted briefly of things domestic and then hung up with expressions of goodwill. David drummed his fingers on the table, recalled his interview with Darrell, and permitted himself a moment of malicious excitement. Never mind losing a battle – there remained the war! He had not yet finished with Dr Darrell.

In such a mood of gleeful enterprise, he telephoned Elizabeth and shared with her his anticipations. As he recited the result of their latest enquiries, Elizabeth was conscious in herself, however, of mounting unease.

'I should be very careful if I were you,' she said at last. 'Both of you.'

'What d'you mean?'

'I mean I should be careful.'

To be stopped in mid-flow of his enthusiasm, even by

Elizabeth, was frustrating. He could not keep an edge of irritation out of his voice.

'Of course we'll be careful. It's our job to be careful.'

'I know that, darling. I'm not saying you aren't careful. It's just that, well, that man Darrell must be incredibly clever.' It was not the most fortunate word to have used and she knew it as soon as it was out.

'Cleverer than I am, you mean?' David could hear the childishness in his own voice and was irritated with himself for it.

'In some ways, yes. Look,' she continued rapidly before he could respond, 'tell me one thing – how did all those people die?'

'All sorts of ways. I've told you. One of leukemia. One of a heart attack. Two by accident. One. . .'

'That's what I'm trying to say. You think Darrell's behind those deaths, don't you?'

'Yes, I do. Don't you?'

'Yes, I do. But, the point is, can you imagine just how one man could organize so many different kinds of death in so many different places?'

'Well, no, I can't. But,'

'So – if Darrell is behind all this, he must be diabolically clever. I'm not trying to put you down, darling. I'm just trying to say, take care. That man frightens me. There's something about this whole thing that's peculiar. Uncanny.'

'Yes, well, I see what you mean.' He was mollified, but not completely. It *was* irritating to have his enthusiasm dampened. 'And anyway,' he grumbled, 'I'm only starting some investigations. Most of it will just be CID checking files, I expect.'

Elizabeth knew that even yet she had not fully succeeded in communicating her feelings about Darrell. She also knew David and herself well enough to suspect that for the moment she could tell him no more. She turned the conversation into other, more tranquil channels and he followed.

Yet, with the receiver replaced, David was still aware of unease and irritation. Elizabeth had communicated more of her feelings than either of them realized and his earlier mood of elation had vanished. He got up and wandered to the window. He was not sure whether he was angry with Elizabeth for affecting him, or himself for letting himself be affected, or Nikos Kakoyannis and James Darrell for starting the whole thing in the first place. He certainly had too much respect for his wife's perceptions simply to write them off. Hmm. He drifted back to the phone, made a note of his calls in Aarons' book, then wandered to the kitchen. Aarons would not be home until late and he was to prepare his own supper. He lit the gas under the kettle and wondered idly what was on television. Confound the woman! Why on earth couldn't she just be an adoring little wife?

Chapter Nine

The Offering

Within twenty-four hours of his return to Salisbury, Darrell received a telegram from the Chairman that summoned him at once back to London. Neither the journey nor the hour was convenient and it was a tired figure, worn already by a long day, who entered the Academy in the late evening and nodded curtly to the pale, bespectacled young woman who sat at an enquiry desk painting her finger nails green.

Minutes later Darrell was knocking discreetly at a heavy oak door on the fifth floor. The door bore a brass plate on which was the one word 'Chairman'. He waited. After a few seconds a green light glowed on his right and he heard from the lock the faintest 'bleep'. He turned the handle and entered.

He had been in this place before and knew what to expect. Heavy oak panelling. Heavy velvet curtains, closely drawn. Deep carpet. Heavy Edwardian furniture. All dimly perceived in the glow of a single table lamp, dark green and bronze, and the flames of a huge fire that glowed and crackled beneath an ornate chimney piece and bathed the room in constantly shifting light. The central heating seemed, as always, to be on full power and combined with the fire to create an atmosphere of stifling warmth.

And yet, as Darrell stood in the doorway, he was aware of a change. Usually, the Chairman was seated behind his desk and received his visitor there. This time the desk was empty and at first Darrell could see his master nowhere. Then a voice from a deep leather armchair in front of the blaze said 'Come.'

Slowly, Darrell advanced.

'Sit.'

This was an unusual honour. Darrell sat in the armchair opposite, his knees almost touching the old man's. Heat from the fire was here quite appalling, and at close quarters the Chairman reeked of sickly sweet perfume that mocked rather than disguised a stench of decay. But Darrell had long since ceased caring whether another's company gave him pleasure in any normal way – physical, emotional, or moral. What mattered was power. And here was a source of it. Clearly, this was to be a special occasion. His heart throbbed with anticipation.

The old man leant forward, scraggy chicken neck craning awkwardly over the stiff Victorian collar.

'You know why I have sent for you?'

'Perhaps.'

'The offering.'

'Yes?' Darrell's voice was slightly breathless.

'Our Master says that you are ready to make it. It shall be part of the Ceremony of Power.'

There was silence. Then the Chairman spoke again. 'The policeman – the one who came to you. He has a woman. No children, but a woman. She shall be the offering. You know what to do?'

'Yes. But – Adam's wife? Surely she won't be – er – virgin.' To his irritation, Darrell (who would have blasphemed the Divine Name without thought) found himself stammering.

'It does not matter. The Power wants her. She is young. Wholesome. On this occasion it will be enough.'

'I see.'

'On All Hallows Eve. It will be a holocaust. The house. Everything. You and I will work it here. Alone. Before the Ceremony. The Ceremony will release it, and it will advance you to Mastery. The others will not know. They are not yet ready.'

The old man laid a bony hand on Darrell's knee. 'It will also be a vengeance, eh? A vengeance on foolish men who interefere, and silly women who marry them.'

His lips stretched in what seemed to be a smile. Even Darrell's heart gave a leap, for that grimace was an invitation to hell. But the hesitation was momentary – an instinctive rebellion of flesh against the fixed determination of will. A second later and James Darrell smiled back. The invitation was accepted. As the old man and the young met each others' gaze, it was suddenly difficult to distinguish between them; or, indeed, to be sure that they were still alive.

The air was heavy with the sharp smell of cheap cigarettes – Embassy Tipped and Player's Number Six. Union Jacks festooned the walls, almost obliterating the fading yellow paintwork. It was strange, reflected Irma Ashliman, what importance men could attach to a piece of coloured rag on a stick. How many different things this one had symbolized – justice, oppression, freedom, bondage. And how desperately important it had become to this group, who clearly found in it a vital symbol in their own quest for identity and purpose. Her eye roamed casually over the dozen or so who sat on folding wooden chairs listening to the oratory of Tom Clanthorpe and occasionally interjecting questions. Two of them, in mid or late fifties, looked and spoke like retired military men. Their tweed sports coats and cavalry twill trousers were old, but well cut and pressed. Their shoes also

were old-fashioned, but polished to brilliance. Six or seven
others were in their late thirties. A few more looked like late
teenagers. Short hair and imitation leather jackets were the
most common uniform. One or two (ridiculously) wore
sunglasses.

'. . . the answer is simple. The repatriation of immigrants
will free vast sums at present tied to Social Services for these
people. That money will be redirected to our own old people.
And what is more. . .'

She looked discreetly at her watch. It was time to be going.
She must at least catch some of the other meeting. She rose
quietly from her chair, and moved to the door. In the narrow,
untidy entrance hall, George and Bill, the two usual 'heavies'
were on watch for the unwanted – left-wing trouble makers
who would be given a thick ear and a quick passage to the
street outside for their pains. George was overweight, with
small eyes, and she felt uncomfortable when he looked at
her. Bill Maclaren, a burly ex-marine in his thirties, was
altogether more pleasant.

'Evening, Mrs Porter. Off early again?'

'I'm afraid so, Bill.'

'The old man keeps you rushing about, does he?'

She laughed. 'Good night, Bill.'

'Good night, Mrs Porter.'

Pigs-eyes, as usual, said nothing, but stared unpleasantly
as she left. Less noticeably, Bill Maclaren's eyes also strayed
after her as she disappeared through the battered swing
doors.

Fifteen minutes later, she pulled up the black Lotus in
Steadman Street and sat for a few minutes doing something
to her hair in the vanity mirror. When she got out, it was
combed straighter then usual and she was wearing thick-
rimmed glasses. She took off the white belted raincoat she
had worn earlier and threw it into the back of the car. Then
she extracted a rather more battered mac of indeterminate

colour and put it on. The result hardly amounted to a disguise but created a change of style that would certainly have confused anyone who attempted to describe her.

The atmosphere at the left-wing meeting was actually not very different from that which she had left. A couple of heavies on the door greeted her as 'Laura'. Inside the hall there were red flags instead of Union Jacks and posters of Che Guevara and Lenin. But the same yellow paint. The same uncomfortable folding chairs. Even the cigarette smoke smelt the same – with maybe a hint of Gauloises. The mix of people was slightly different – younger, and including several women. Blue denim rather than black leather was the uniform. And there were (thank God) no sunglasses. In other words, everything looked as usual. Good. She moved a chair at the back to a place where she could see better and sat down. Why exactly she kept this personal watch on her cells, she was not sure. She could have worked only through her agents, as did Danby and Darrell. In many ways, it was safer. But somehow, she preferred this personal check. It kept her in touch. She settled herself to listen.

Chapter Ten

Michael Aarons

Michael Aarons drove his car into the vicarage garden and got out to close the gates. He was tired. He had spent the evening at All Saints, Margaret Street, lecturing to the Institute on 'The Essence of Barthian Dogmatics'. Apparently it had gone well. There had been, in his view, good questions, and one particularly interesting person had stayed behind to talk for half an hour. So his efforts had been rewarded. But tiring, all the same!

For Aarons, to speak of theology was always joy, though his path to that joy had not been easy. His first faith in the God of his fathers had perished beyond recall, so it seemed at the time, in the death camp that destroyed his parents and his sisters. Holocaust. Even now, it was hard to find word or shape for that experience. Life, hope, and religion – all overwhelmed. The world – nothing, save hunger, exhaustion, and despair. Then came the death of Steiner. Why that death should have been important to him among so many was never clear, but he had known Josef Steiner as a boy in Vienna (another life, another world!), and in some sense had a part in his end. Josef was a big, gentle lad, naturally clumsy. One day, whilst Aarons was near, that clumsiness

irritated a group of the Latvian SS who controlled the camp
(and, so it then seemed to Aarons, the universe). They killed
him, rather slowly. As they did so, one of them seized Aarons
and threatened to kill him too if he would not shout insults
in chorus with them as Steiner died. So he had shouted, and
could hear himself now – *Jüdische Schwein! Jüdische
Schwein!* – to the background of their laughter and Steiner's
screams. They would probably have killed Aarons anyway
but something distracted them. So they threw him in a corner
and left.

For Michael Aarons, to have jeered at this dying man, his
fellow Jew, was the end. Worse than the excrement. Worse
than the loss of faith. The nadir of humiliation. Yet out of
it blossomed defiance. This was the way things were. This
was the way he was. Then damn them all. Come what may,
if it were by any means possible, Michael Aarons would
survive.

He survived. In many ways he perceived himself as unusual, even amongst that rare band. Most who survived did
so, it seemed to him, because a passion held them fast: a
passion to witness to what had happened, to be faithful, so
giving spark to the unyielding determination that alone could
maintain the disciplines that made survival possible – daily
recitation of the Shema, or the willingness, despite exhaustion and gnawing hunger, to keep back a little tasteless coffee
for a sign of washing. Aarons lacked any commitment, save
perhaps to life itself. A determination that he would not be
beaten. Yet somehow, for him, it was enough. He survived.
Physically, he survived. Emotionally and spiritually, he returned as a dead man to Vienna.

It was over. He had fought for life, and he had won. Now,
whether he liked it or not, life must be lived. The land of
Israel – eretz-Yisroel – might have drawn him once, but no
more. The very passion that naturally inclined him to that
precious soil was a quality that he could not or dare not face.

What then? For a few dangerous months he had wavered, the chaotic society of post-war Vienna matching and rein- forcing the chaos of his own soul. Crime. Drugs. Smuggling. Even the black arts had tempted him briefly. Yet always something held him back. If the death camp had taught him anything, it was that life itself depended upon a degree of decency in common, a social commitment, even where per- sonal commitment was impossible. If you cheated another, or stole his bread, you died. That was not a decree of the SS. It was decreed by the inmates. Only thus could they live. The temptations by which he was now assailed fitted well with his sense of futility; but they also struck at those same last-ditch values by which he and his companions had main- tained life at all. So, at last, he simply found work. He joined an international company that was profiting and expanding in the post-war boom. Being intelligent and cultured, he progressed easily enough. Soon, he was holding a responsible executive position. Then came the offer of promotion, and with it the requirement that he move to England. Having no attachment that mattered to him in Vienna or anywhere else, he came, little dreaming as he splashed across wet tarmac at Heathrow airport, that he had arrived in a new homeland.

From the first, he found in England a measure of tran- quillity. He made a few friends. Read some books. Acquired his first cat. Even brought himself to write an account of his experience in the death camp for the archives of the Yad va Shem, Museum of the Holocaust, in Jerusalem – containing all he could remember that might be useful. Yet through it all – futility. He could hope for nothing, since there was nothing to hope for. He believed nothing, for there was nothing to believe. He felt as little as possible, since to feel was ultimately to face a terrible and growing guilt – that he should be alive at all, when Steiner and all those others were dead.

The process by which he was moved from that desert

seemed to him, looking back, to be a miracle, too subtle in form for precise recollection. Only certain moments stood out. An occasion when a print of El Greco's *Agony of Christ* strangely moved him. A conversation with an American soldier on a train. A battered copy of the Gospel according to Saint Luke, in Luther's version, discovered on a market stall, and read, half with repugnance, half with fascination – like the first encounter of groom and bride.

Then one day he fell upon his bed and wept – tears of grief and joy that wracked his body in an ecstasy, loosing all the passion he had denied since Steiner died. He seemed at once to be in the death camp and on Calvary, hearing a cry that embraced himself and his captors and Steiner and all the world – *Vater, vergib ihnen!* Father, forgive them! In that moment, Michael Aarons believed that he who was Lord on Calvary would be Lord also in that other place. And in that moment, he knew himself a Christian.

There are passions of the heart, and there are passions of the mind, too – especially for a man like Aarons. After the rapture of love given and received, there was zeal to explore the world made new, to ask its meaning, and how he should speak of his joy. That zeal remained. To teach and talk theology was for him the work of love. But still a work! He sighed, and fumbled for his keys, preparing to be greeted with rapturous purring by the cats, and, if not quite with rapture, at least with a degree of reasonable pleasure by his young friend.

Some fifteen minutes later, Michael Aarons and David Adam sat quietly over drinks, enjoying the closing minutes of the day. Little was said, for both men were full of their own thoughts. One thing, however, Aarons did remember.

'That notebook of yours – I looked at it this morning. Actually, you gave me quite a job! It was obviously full of quotations from something mystical and medieval, but I had to check with a good friend, a Rabbi at the Reform Synagogue, to be sure what.'

'I'm sorry. I didn't mean to cause you a lot of trouble.'

'Not trouble – we enjoy a chase! Harold helps me with obscure rabbinics, and I help him with obscure patristics. If they're too obscure for both of us, we commend them to the good God and stop worrying. Anyway – your book. It consists, as I suspected, of extracts from the *Zohar*. Mostly Aramaic. Some Hebrew. I've made a note of the references, if you want them. Obviously, we didn't have time to check every syllable, but so far as we could see, the passages had just been copied out. No comments or notes. Just the text. Rather odd, really. Did it come up in a case?'

'Oh – er – yes. A case.' It was not simply professional etiquette that made David hesitate to say more, for he would have trusted Aarons with anything. The fact was, at present the whole subject was depressing to him and he felt reluctant to talk about it. For his part, Aarons would not have dreamt of probing his friend about a case.

'Ah, well.' His eyes twinkled. 'Obviously you have mystical criminals in your part of the world.'

Both men laughed.

With an effort, David pulled himself together. The priest and the rabbi had gone to some trouble. The least he could do was avail himself of the help they offered. 'Would you believe it if a man told you he'd lent those notes to someone at a conference on philosophy and science?'

'I might,' said Aarons. 'I suppose it would depend on what I thought of him. But I should be puzzled. I don't really understand what the book would be for. If somebody wanted the texts, there are editions. Why work with something written out by hand? I find that very hard to explain. Unless there is some significance in the arrangement, or the selection. We couldn't see any.'

David nodded. That certainly seemed to be a point – a

question worth putting to Darrell, if the chance came. Though David did not doubt he would produce a smooth answer.

'Harold's lent me an English translation,' said the priest. 'If I give you the references, perhaps you should check the passages yourself. You may see something we missed.'

David nodded again. 'Yes. I'll do that. But at any rate there's nothing in them on the surface that seems at all, well – sinister or criminal to you?'

'Not unless you're a devotee of the Rambam,' said Michael Aarons with a chuckle.

'What?'

'I'm sorry.' Aarons' apology was sincere. 'You must forgive an old man trying to be funny. The Rambam – Maimonides – was a medieval scholar. Very reasonable and enlightened. Tried to make us Jews intellectually respectable! The *Zohar* is generally reckoned to be in the opposite camp. That's all! But, seriously, there is nothing sinister or criminal in that notebook in any sense that you or I use the words. At least, not so far as we could see.'

David nodded again. So Kakoyannis' notebook looked like being a blank. Always assuming it was Kakoyannis' notebook. After all, Darrell had had it – how long? A day? Two days? Long enough to forge a substitute? Was the thing they were examining simply an enormous red herring? If only the police had looked at it more closely before letting it out of their hands in the first place! Still, there was no helping that.

He looked up at Aarons. 'Well, thank you,' he said. 'It doesn't get me much farther, but thank you all the same. And perhaps you'll thank your friend for me.'

Aarons smiled, and inclined his head in acknowledgement.

Chapter Eleven

All Hallows Eve

Elizabeth clattered to the front door with milk-bottles, and blinked at the early morning sun. In the night there had been rain. Bushes and paths were soaking. Now the skies were clear, and she breathed an exquisite, exhilarating freshness. Marvellous! And convenient, too – for today was a visiting day, and it was always more pleasant in the sun.

She was about to close the door when her attention was caught by something fluttering on it, low down. She bent, and examined it. A roughly torn triangle of paper, fastened with a drawing pin. She withdrew the pin (it came easily enough) and peered at the paper. On it, what looked like writing. In a strange script. A child's code? A foreign language? She had no idea. Yet someone had taken the trouble to pin it there. How very odd!

The kettle whistled, and with half-conscious resolve to 'show it to David' Elizabeth pushed the paper on to the hall table and went back to the kitchen. Splodger sniffed anxiously at the bottom of the door, then trotted after her, curled tail bobbing. Pooh followed with more measured tread.

Darrell drew to a close his account of the Department's work and noted that his three visitors from the Ministry of Defence were impressed. He cared little. Entertaining senior military men was an irritation on any day and especially on this. He had returned to Salisbury very late the previous night. Already this morning he had been up since four, and had surreptitiously visited the Adams' house. Creeping around other people's gardens in damp darkness was not an experience he relished, but the task could not, by its nature, be delegated. He would have valued, following it, a morning of scientific calm. Instead – there in the diary was the appointment, made months before, when an opportunity to impress the Ministry had seemed worth taking. The whole thing was now so far from his chief concerns that he could scarcely conceive the state of mind in which it had been important.

As it was he might have ducked out at the last minute or sent a substitute, had he received even the briefest notice. But he had already been late when he reached the Centre, and the men were waiting. Habit dies hard and, suppressing his fury, he had proceeded to dazzle them. It was, indeed, easy enough. What he actually told them (what, to speak plainly, they could understand) was child's play; any of his research students could have said as much – or even an intelligently briefed commentator from the BBC. The trick, of course, was that he was none of these things, but the senior man with the brilliant reputation – who obviously knew so much more than he could tell. He showed them the QZ Room ('Kew-zee' to his American colleagues) where a number of experiments (none of them particularly important, but all spectacular) were permanently set up to impress the enquirer; he showed them video tape of new work in Europe; he spoke concisely and convincingly of the advantages of biological attack over conventional warfare, including nuclear. (The military men were aware of the arguments here, and nodded sagely. It did no harm to let them feel reasonably intelligent about something.) Someone asked a question about co-operation with Fort Detrick. Someone else was even well-informed enough to quote from Fritz Haber – 'a higher form of killing' – and he acknowledged the terrible phrase graciously. Finally, he sketched briefly, in layman's language, a few of the biological principles and problems involved.

He paused. Abruptly, he was moved to go further, to say what they would not (he felt sure) have heard before, but might soon have cause to remember. 'And yet,' he continued, 'all that we have said regarding biological mutation can, and must, be set in a much wider context if it is properly to be understood.' He looked round the room. Someone absently stubbed out a cigarette. 'Consider, if you will, the concept of cybernetics. Cybernetics means control. The science of control. A plastic key in your wife's washing-machine, and it washes according to one programme rather than another. A card punched with holes, and an electronic computer supervises a process. So much for the principle. Yet our most sophisticated achievements to date in this field – indeed, the most sophisticated achievements we can even envisage – are simplicity itself, compared to the technology with which Nature confronts us – a technology upon which all that we have been examining this morning is totally dependent.'

Carried along by the flow of thought, he addressed his audience without pause. 'All living things appear to derive their characteristics from those tiny cells, the genes, of which we have been speaking. Those genes, as we have seen, determine species, sex, even the colour of eyes and hair. They are, in fact, the archetypal computer cards. What then? When we build a control system for a process – any process – it is axiomatic that the speed of the control system must be greater than the speed of the process controlled. You can mow your lawn without smashing into the garden shed because you think faster than the lawn-mower works. That being so, the programming of matter for the creation of living beings must be achieved by a control process faster than the life process. A process able to convey and impose information that itself controls the life process. A process sufficiently superior in intelligence to us, to be able to programme our intelligence. Have we any idea what such a process might be, or what might be our relationship to it?'

There was a curious silence. It was the Admiral who spoke. 'Are you talking about God, Dr Darrell?'

James Darrell smiled. He had enjoyed watching their faces and was, for the moment, in a mood to be patient. And the question was not, actually, a bad one, for a beginner. 'No, I am not talking about God – at least, not in any traditional sense. Though I would certainly affirm that certain human experiences and observations, hitherto largely written off as superstition, may need re-appraisal – the ancient Peruvians' *huaca*, the American Indians' *orenda*, and so on – but, basically, gentlemen, I am not speaking of metaphysics, but of scientific observation and its implications. If there is a 'god' involved, then it is a 'god' of this world – and what we know of it is to do with intelligence, power, and control.'

'And what do you see as the importance of this?' asked the Admiral.

'The importance is this. We are concerned, as a nation – indeed, as a species – with success. With power. With survival. That is why you are here. That is why Her Majesty's government finances this establishment. And observation points us, if we take it seriously, in the direction where success, power, and survival lie. Intelligence and control. An intelligent nation will control a backward nation – even without wishing to. Intelligent individuals will control backward individuals. That is the pattern of life itself, for intelligence controls the universe. That is what observation shows us. And its implications are, I suggest, far wider than merely the creation of new weapons. Its implications call in question the whole social and political order of which we are part.'

There was a discreet knock at the door.

'Come in,' said Darrell. A junior colleague entered, and gave him a note. He glanced at it, and nodded.

'Gentlemen, the Director wishes us to attend him for drinks in the bar. I am sure I have taken up quite enough of your time.'

'Good heavens, no!'

'Not at all.'

'Most interesting.'

A spell seemed to fall from the group. Chairs were pushed back and general conversation resumed. With James Darrell leading, they headed for the bar. Only the Admiral was silent. Somewhere, he sensed an unanswered question.

It was the second (and concluding) day of the trial that had brought David Adam to London. Justice was done in the Queen's name, and at three o'clock he was free of responsibility. Not that he felt irresponsible. Quite the contrary. Burdened by a vague sense of depression, he wandered back to St Andrew's.

There, as Aarons suggested, he decided to read through the extracts from the *Zohar* in the translation provided by the rabbi. He went up to Michael's study. Five large volumes were stacked on the desk. On top of them was a pencilled note:

> Dear David,
> Here are the references
> – please be careful. These
> books are something of a
> treasure!
> Ever yours,
> Michael.

There followed a list of passages and pages.

He sat down, and took the first volume from the pile. It

was not difficult to see what the priest meant. The blue leather binding was beautiful. He opened the flyleaf, and was further informed:

> This edition of the Zohar is
> limited to 1250 sets of twelve
> volumes, Volume I being numbered
> 1 to 1250, and 48 special sets
> printed on Banham Green's hand-
> made paper, volume I of which
> is signed by the translators and
> numbered I to XLVIII.

Beneath, the number of the copy and the two autographs,

> H. Sperling
> M. Simon

written (he suspected) with steel nibs.

Feeling slightly self-conscious, he got to his feet, went to the bathroom, washed his hands, and returned. Now – for the list!

In the next two hours, he perhaps learnt something of the experience of Israel ('As the lily among thorns is tinged with red and white, so the community of Israel is visited now with justice and now with mercy'), and even something of the nature of Godhead ('For all things are in Him and He is in all things: He is both manifest and concealed: manifest in order to uphold the whole, and concealed for He is found nowhere'). Concerning Darrell's works and plans he learnt, of course, nothing.

At half-past five, the telephone rang. It was Elizabeth. Their conversation refreshed him, though not completely. As if by unspoken agreement, no mention was made of James Darrell.

Since it was to be David's last evening in London, Aarons had arranged to be at home. Though normally relying on a housekeeper, Aarons was himself a fine cook and occasionally enjoyed using this talent for his friends. This was such an occasion. The housekeeper had been given the evening off. David and the cats were (in much the same tone of voice) banished from the kitchen and Michael Aarons proceeded to create. Later, they sat down at the table. To begin with, there was a delicate mushroom salad, perfect to provoke the appetite. When that was eaten, the priest filled their glasses with a bold red wine from the grapes of Mount Carmel, and produced – *Tzimmes*!

'*Tzimmes* means excitement!' he delcared, bearing a tightly closed pot to the table. 'Now – smell!' He lifted the lid and at once the room was filled with a rich, spicy fragrance.

'This,' said David after eating a little, 'is incredible. Marvellous! How on earth do you do it?'

'There are as many ways to make a *Tzimmes* as there are *bubbes* to invent them,' replied Aarons. 'Some like it more savoury. Some sweeter. This is *my* way – and certainly, I'll show you afterwards if you want. But then you and Elizabeth must invent your own!'

After the *Tzimmes*, a cheesecake. 'Milk and honey, to remind us of the Promised Land,' observed Aarons.

Some time later, contentedly seated before an excellent fire (the first of the year) and sipping strong black coffee (freshly ground and made in a jug, for Aarons would brook no nonsense with percolators) David had to admit that his friend had excelled himself. He glanced at Aarons, seated opposite.

'It's good?' asked the priest.

'It's very good!'

Aarons chuckled. There was silence, save for the crackle of logs. Both men sat gazing peacefully into the flames.

Tom Wardle walked to the end of the platform with a hundred or so others who had alighted from the Leeds to Kings Cross train, and glanced around him. A hoarding caught his eye. 'Top people read "The Times"!' They would! He silently cursed all top people, and then looked at his watch. 8.06. On time, for once. Well, that was something. Time for a drink. No sense in getting there before he had to. Poncing about with those creeps. Somebody had said something about fasting, but to hell with that for a lark. If he was going to be damned, he'd as soon be damned drunk as sober.

Sitting in the Kings Cross Station buffet a few minutes later, he gazed at the chaos of hoardings, locomotives, and humanity in front of him, and sipped his second pint. What the hell was he in all this for anyway? Why not go back? The next train? Be shot of the whole lot of them? For a moment, the glorious vista opened. Then – he remembered the Chairman. And trembled. The Chairman knew too many things. Too much of the past. God alone knew what he'd do if he were let down. It didn't bear thinking about. And anyway (a certain dogged competitiveness came to his aid) was he going to be beaten by that little ponce Darrell? Have Irma Ashliman laughing at him up her fancy sleeve? He squared his shoulders and drank again. He'd started this and he'd bloody well go through with it. He looked again at his watch. Time for another. Thank God the train had been on time.

'Adam in London? But that ruins everything.'

'Not at all. I have known he was in London all the time. All that matters is the woman. If anything, the man's absence is advantageous to us.'

'Advantageous?'

'They are both – believers, of a sort. In certain circumstances, two such combined can cause considerable delay.

Alone, she certainly cannot last long. It will be so much easier.'

'And the woman alone will be enough?'

'Of course it will be enough. She is the offering. I have said. She is young, intelligent, healthy. The fruit she might have borne, the purposes she would have fulfilled – all lost. It is quite satisfactory. The man, if you will, can be destroyed at leisure. Perhaps after he has sufficiently savoured her death.'

'You're sure?'

The Chairman said nothing and Darrell bit his lip. The question was superfluous. Then the Chairman spoke again, 'You have what is necessary?'

Eagerly, Darrell produced what he had been instructed to acquire – oddments gleaned from the Adams' house and its environs. Paint from a gate. A piece of cement chipped from between bricks. Small items of clothing stolen from a clothes line. He and the Chairman considered the pathetic remnants with utter gravity.

'It is enough. You left the talisman?'

'Pinned to the door.'

'Then I shall prepare the chalice. Kneel.'

James Darrell sank to his knees and prepared to make his dedication.

Chapter Twelve

The Opinions of the Archdeacon

David put down his cup, and spoke on impulse. 'Have you ever come across something called the Academy for Philosophical Studies?' he asked.

Aarons looked keenly at him. 'You mean a group in Bayswater?'

'That's right – in Bayswater. Off the Bayswater Road. You know about them?'

'A little, yes. Why? You're not thinking of joining them, are you?'

'Good Lord, no. It's to do with something that came up in a case. Something I'm checking. But it could be important. If you felt free – professionally free, I mean – to say how you felt about them, I should like to know.'

'Would you?' Something like anger flickered across the older man's face, and when he spoke again, it seemed to be with a conscious effort at restraint. 'I must confess,' he said at last, 'that I find the Academy rather tiresome. Some of us seem to spend quite a lot of time with its failures.'

'Failures?'

'Yes.'

'Can you tell me what kind of failures?'

Again, in Aarons' manner there was the apparent determination to be reasonable. 'Well – it's a group that seems to expect certain very rigid mental and spiritual standards from those who go far with it. In return, it offers rewards. Those who cannot maintain the standards tend to find the experience, well, depressing. And some of us have had to help.'

'You and other clergy?'

'Oh – not all clergy by any means. I've a friend who's a psychiatrist. Another who's a GP. Cases have come through the Samaritans. All sorts of people have been involved.'

'Hmm.'

'Sometimes there's a financial side to things, as well. I must be careful what I say here. I'm not saying I've any evidence of them doing anything actually illegal,' ('No one ever has,' thought David gloomily.) 'but like other groups (including, of course, the Christian church) the Academy does look for financial and material commitment from its members. A few people seem to have got themselves into difficulty. To be fair, when the Academy has been told, they've always cancelled covenants, even refunded money. But you know how threatened and irrational people become when they feel themselves under pressure.'

'Yes,' said David grimly, 'I do.' (He knew door-to-door salesmen with the same technique. They were always willing to refund when confronted, of course. That was what made them so hard to catch.)

David was reluctant to ask his next question, since it might appear to press the priest too far. Yet it seemed important to be as clear as possible about what Aarons was saying. 'Would you feel able to tell me how many of these people there are – people you and your friends are helping? I mean – just roughly? Is it sort of – two or three a year? Or a dozen or so?'

'You realize I could not possibly reveal to you the names or details of these people?'

'I realize that.'

Aarons nodded. 'Then there seems no reason why you should not have some idea of the figure.' There was a pause, whilst he did a mental calculation. 'So far as I can recall, we are at present working with twenty-five people. I will tell you that a sister in one of our orders has had eleven cases passed to her alone since the summer.'

Twenty-five. Out of the millions who populate London, not many. Yet, considering the small size of the Academy, more than enough. Nor was there any clear reason to assume that Aarons and his friends were the only people helping the Academy's former members. Perhaps there were more? On the other hand, perhaps the Academy tended to attract neurotic, depressive people? Wouldn't that account for a high number of such people amongst its failures?

Aarons occasionally displayed a disconcerting ability to answer the unasked question. 'I think I am free to tell you,' he observed, 'that of the cases I have mentioned, only two appear to have any previous history of mental breakdown. They may not have been the happiest or most integrated people in the world before they came to the Academy, but they seem at least to have coped with life. That is more than they can do now.'

David nodded. What Michael said about the Academy confirmed feelings he already had. But the stronger those feelings became, the more he was presented with another question. Why? If the Academy was involved in some way with all those deaths that surrounded Darrell, to say nothing of the mental breakdowns and personal disasters of which Michael spoke – then why? What was the Academy after?

'Why d'you think they're doing all this?' he said at last. 'I mean – what's in it for the Academy?'

Aarons fetched the jug and poured out more coffee before

answering. Then he said, 'I can't give you an answer that will be of use in an English court, or even in your policeman's notebook. I can, if you wish, give you my opinion of the reasoning behind their actions, stated in my own terms, for what that is worth.'

'I should like that very much.'

'Very well.' Aarons sighed, and paused. He was about to be judgmental, and that was not a thing he found easy at any time. (Had he not jeered at Steiner's death?) 'I believe,' he said at last, 'that at the core of the Academy is a group of men and women with an approach to life that I should call 'gnostic.' That is to say, they seek salvation through knowledge, particularly knowledge of the supernatural – what they (I think) would call 'spiritual' knowledge. More immediately, they seek power through such knowledge. Because they know, they will be strong. Because they understand, they will be able to use, perhaps even to control.'

David was listening intently.

'Don't misunderstand me. I admit that religion does have to do with becoming in some senses stronger – at least it has to do with becoming fuller, more complete, more truly human. But I would say that even those things are not basically what religion is about. It's like marriage. A good marriage will make you stronger, too. But you being stronger is not what marriage is about. Marriage is about trust and hope and forgiveness between people. But you know that better than I.

'The same, I believe, is true of religion. True religion is about trust and hope and forgiveness in our relationship with God. It's about that kind of seeking for the transcendent that desires a love without end, and a true fatherhood. Gnosticism is false religion, because it does not desire relationship, but mastery. Not forgiveness, but power. I think it is because those who run the Academy care only for power, that they feel able to treat quite ruthlessly those who cannot keep the pace they set. They will use them, and they will cast them aside, as they choose. In their eyes the weak have no value, save as food for the strong.'

Aarons was silent. 'You asked what I thought was the Academy's purpose. Do I answer your question?'

David nodded slowly. 'Yes, I think you do. But – can people get power this way? I mean, real power,' (he thought of the men who had died twenty years ago) 'I mean, power, say, to kill people?'

'I suppose that will depend on how far they go. If you deal with a marriage or a friendship only for what you get out of it, you do get something. Power. Satisfaction. Something of the sort. Though of course in doing that you do not have any real relationship with your wife or your friend. If you try to deal with religion like that, I don't doubt you get something, too, and are in touch with something – though hardly God. There is a long tradition of rebellious forces in the universe ready to make use of rebellious men. Yes. You will get something. For a while. In the end, of course, it is nonsense.'

'Nonsense?'

'Oh yes, I think so. This quest for power, for control. To use religion for our own ends – what does it finally mean but that we are trying to be gods? Little gods! Like the story of Adam – 'You shall be as God, knowing good and evil'. And certainly it is nonsense. The most ridiculous of all nonsense. There are times, I must admit, when to live and feel that there is no God anywhere – that is not unreasonable. But to suppose that *I* am God!' He shrugged.

'The tail wagging the dog.'

'As you say,' (Aarons smiled) 'the tail wagging the dog. The irony is,' he added, 'that I believe in the end the promise is that we shall be like God – sharers in the divine nature. But that, like life itself, will be a gift. Not something we win through our own cleverness.'

The fire had burned low in the grate, and David watched as Aarons made it up.

'If the church feels as strongly as this about things like the Academy,' he said at last, 'why doesn't it speak out about them?'

'You mean denounce them?' Aarons shook his head. 'I don't think the church is in a very good position to denounce anyone. The joy and the hope of the church are that she has been given a holy thing, a promise. But as human beings, aren't we as corruptible as any? Haven't we tried to use God for our own ends? Haven't we practised false religion?'

'That sounds to me like saying you can't say something's wrong, because you once did it yourself.'

Aarons nodded, conceding his friend's point. 'Yes. I see what you mean. Perhaps we should speak out more boldly. Perhaps you are right. But if so – then only as fellow penitents. Not denouncing the thing as if we had no taint of it. That would be terrible.' He paused. 'In this case, there are practical difficulties. Even assuming we chose to speak and anyone chose to listen – not something we can assume, by the way – of what do we speak? Of the poor souls who come to us? But that would betray the very confidence they place in us. Then what evidence do we have? What real evidence? Do you have evidence? Evidence that will save you from an accusation of libel in an English court?'

'Not yet, though I'm trying to get it.'

There was another pause. David felt that in some way he had sidetracked himself, and returned to his main theme. 'At any rate, you personally regard this thing, this false religion, as dangerous?'

'I regard it as diabolic.'

'Diabolic?'

'It takes the best, and corrupts it. To use sex or politics as weapons of control is bad enough, but to use religion!

That is the most evil of all. If it is not our best that we do in God's name, then it will certainly be our worst.'

'Oh.' Just when he felt that the subject was almost exhausted, the word 'diabolic' for some reason disturbed him. 'Then you're not actually accusing the Academy of devil worship or anything like that?'

'As for that,' Aarons shrugged, 'I don't know. Certainly people have said strange things, but – I don't know.'

A number of thoughts were, however, coming together in David's mind. The scene in the cathedral. The foul-smelling candles and the dead old man. He'd been worshipping the devil, hadn't he. And what about that inexplicable trail of death surrounding Darrell? And the fear in Elizabeth's voice? Now at last he sensed what she had sensed. Diabolic. Wasn't that the word she had used? Diabolically clever. That's what she had said. What in God's name was he up against – he with his police procedures and his plodding common sense? Mr Plod the policeman. Did even Michael Aarons really know what was going on in the Academy?

'Tell me – what would you do if you thought you were up against witchcraft, the devil, the real thing, I mean?' The question was blurted out.

Aarons looked sharply at him, then answered slowly and with great care. 'First,' he said, 'I should try not to take my own role in the matter too seriously. If the devil is to be defeated (and he is), then it will not be by you, nor by a thousand better than you. As a Christian, you live in confidence that God himself has already won the only victory that matters, in Christ. Please don't misunderstand me. I'm not saying that evil isn't both frightening and horrible. Shouldn't I know better than that? I'm not saying, don't be careful and brave, when you have to fight it. But I am saying, remember before all else, that Satan is ridiculous, and his rebellion a pathetic absurdity. Don't let all those silly modern books about battles between demons and clergymen deceive you.

Nothing – in life or death, in heaven or earth or under the earth – can finally separate you from God's love. Not even, if we knew it, in the valley of shadow.' (*Jüdische schwein! Jüdische schwein!*) 'Even there,' he whispered softly, 'you are with me.' There was a pause. 'Do you believe that?'

David, who had been contemplating the fire, looked up slowly, and met the eye of his host. A faint, unintentioned smile flickered across his face. 'Yes,' he said, 'I think perhaps I do. Something like that, anyway.'

Again, silence.

David actually felt very much better. Better than he had felt for days. A release of tension. Then, suddenly, 'Look, I don't really want to talk about this any more. Not for the moment, anyway. I think I need to go to bed. Do you mind?'

'Of course I don't mind. Are you all right?'

'Oh yes. I'm all right. In fact I feel fine. It's just that, somehow, I seem to want to sleep.'

'Well then, good. Is there anything you need?'

'Nothing at all. Really. I'm fine. And thank you – for the dinner and – everything. It was great.'

'Good. Well – good-night then. Sleep well.'

'Good-night, Michael. And thanks again. Oh,' (David, already half-way to the door paused again, and the awkward smile reappeared) 'Look, I don't want to sound dramatic or anything, and I really am all right. But – if you were to pray for me, I think I'd appreciate it. The fact is, there's something I'm involved in. I'm not quite sure what I'm up against.'

Aarons nodded. 'Of course I will pray for you. And by the way – if your Academy is involved in Satanism, then tonight we should pray for them also.'

'Tonight? Why tonight?'

'Don't you know the date?'

'Er – October the thirty-first.'

'That's right. All Hallows Eve. By tradition the night when the powers of darkness attempt their worst.'

'Oh. The witches' festival and all that?'

'Exactly.'

'Hmm. Yes. I suppose I had heard of that – I just didn't connect it with this. Well, certainly, I take the point. For them too.' (Another pause.) 'Good-night, then.'

'Good-night.'

Aarons continued to sit and watch the fire. After a while, he put down his coffee-cup, got to his feet, and made sure that the fire was safe. He walked across to the wide, handsome window (whose curtains were still not drawn, though it was now dark) and gazed out, contemplating benignly the elegant seventeenth-century silhouette of the church tower and, beyond it, the monstrous blaze of the Daily Mirror building. At last he turned away, glanced round the room and went to his desk for keys. A few minutes later he was walking slowly down the stairs, through the connecting passage and into the church.

Chapter Thirteen

The Summons

It seemed to David that he slept immediately on getting into bed. A sleep without dreams. Now, in an instant, he was awake, his nerves tingling with a strange, undefined excitement. He sat up and looked round the room. The curtains were not fully drawn, and he could see between them the arc of the moon in her first quarter. He looked at his watch. A quarter to eleven. He had slept for less than an hour. Yet he did not feel in the least like sleeping again. More like going for a walk. Perhaps he would read for a bit.

Then he had his idea. To look at the Academy. It was absurd, when he came to think of it, that he had spent so much time worrying about the Academy and had never actually seen the building. It should be easy enough to find. And maybe he'd spot something. Or think of a plan. A new approach. That was it. He'd go and look at the Academy. He switched on the bedside light, got quickly out of bed, and reached for his clothes.

Downstairs, he realized that Aarons had gone into the church. It seemed a pity to disturb him. He hesitated a moment, then scribbled a note describing his sudden urge for midnight adventure and left it on the hall table. A few minutes later, having gently closed the vicarage gates behind him, he was turning his car towards a deserted Holborn Circus. His feelings of excitement moderated to a calm, almost relaxed concentration on the next task. The hands of the illuminated church clock pointed precisely to eleven. Ahead of him, the equestrian figure of Albert Prince Consort continued to raise its hat in the direction of Holborn Viaduct. To his right, the windows of St Andrew's Lady Chapel shone brightly, and through them could be glimpsed the copper lamp that hangs before the altar. The lights in front of him changed to green, and he pressed the accelerator.

Elizabeth put down her book and looked at her watch, wondering whether to go to bed early. It had not, from her point of view, been a good day. None of her cases had gone well and she had come home at four with feelings of frustration and a slight headache. The headache had gone but the feelings had not. Compounding it all was the anxiety she still felt about David's pursuit of James Darrell – though she had carefully avoided mentioning the matter when they talked again on the phone. Why was she anxious? She really did not know. And she hated talk about 'woman's intuition'. Certainly, it looked as if Darrell and the Academy were dangerous – but then, so were lots of the people with whom David dealt. And clever, too. And as he had said, he was only asking people to check files and ask questions. It wasn't as if he were going after Darrell with a gun. The fact remained, she wished to goodness that they had never heard of Darrell. And particularly that she'd not encouraged David to pursue the thing. She picked up her book, read five lines, then put it down. This was absurd. Perhaps a bath would do something for her mood. A long, luxurious bath. She contemplated the prospect for a few seconds, nodded, and uncurled herself from the armchair.

Once again, like the stirring of a memory, Sabrina was moved by a longing to escape. This time there was a difference. The former longing had been tinged and modified with other emotions, guilt amongst them, her keeper's 'Thou shalt not' beating into her heart. The ardour she now felt was without guilt; wholly righteous, wholly zealous, as if the truest and most perfect of all keepers summoned and must be obeyed. She rose, tail sweeping from side to side, ears pricked, her whole being tense with collected power.

The gate swung silently back at the touch of her paw. Electronic gadgetry had failed, precisely (as it happened) as the young woman predicted it might. Someone had forgotten the button. But of course no question of this entered Sabrina's consciousness, only pure joy in obedience, pure urge to depart, and pure animal passion, before which the matter of electronic locks was merely, and properly, irrelevant.

Silent and powerful, she loped between cages, north-east towards the main gate. Perhaps, as she went, she was cautious. If so, then it was by an instinct at that moment secondary, for no knowledge was in her other than her need to answer the one who called, and to answer now. Once she paused and scented the wind, nostrils twitching, then trotted on, a dark shadow moving purposefully and quickly between the enclosures.

James Darrell had dedicated himself to the offering. Now he and the Chairman left the study and joined their colleagues in a dark temple that formed the upper floor of the Academy. The Chairman stood before the altar; the others flanked him. The place stank of oil, of blood and death. Heavy velvet dulled the sound of their incantation. Oil lamps burned with a sickly unease. Circling the temple, the five cast incense on their fires; then, bowing low, adored.

In the Outer Circle Road of Regent's Park, David sat in his small car, the engine running, and swore. Damn it, what was he thinking of? He prided himself (though a provincial) on his knowledge of London. Why on earth had he turned right in Southampton Row instead of going on towards Marble Arch? Still more absurd – what had possessed him to drive round Park Crescent and into the Outer Circle? He was now not sure how to get back to the Bayswater Road at all. And where the blazes was the A to Z?

As his hand fumbled under the dashboard, feeling for the map, there was a sharp, insistent scratching at the nearside door. Now what? Leaning further across, he opened it. For a moment he saw nothing, then felt a surge of fear at the huge creature who reared out of the darkness. Sabrina flowed in with surprising grace for her size, and settled, dog-like, on a back seat scarcely large enough to hold her. David looked at her in amazement, and she looked back. Then a noise from the road – a passing car – attracted her attention, and she turned her head, revealing to his astonished gaze the almost healed scar on her left ear. Another picture flowed into his mind. A desecrated sanctuary. A body. Scattered belongings. A wolf, *bleeding from the left ear*. And in that instant, David remembered. His heart missed a beat and the hair rose on the back of his neck. It was surely the same. The wolf from the cathedral. The bane of Nikos Kakoyannis. And now she had found him. But how on earth. . . ? The wolf continued to look, watching him with simple expectancy, head on one side, ears pricked. Fur, breath, and smell of the earth – she filled the car with her presence. He was touched, incongruously, with a sense of the ridiculous. It was almost as if she were asking for a walk! What was she asking? What was he to do?

Then, it happened. His senses, his thoughts, his fears – all were overwhelmed. It seemed that the sheer being of everything round him – the metal and glass of the car, the creaking plastic, the beast – the glorious beast! – all pressed upon him and offered him knowledge. He and they were caught and transfigured in a field of force, a communion, a being, a person, a divine breath. And in it and through it – he knew.

It was over. The wolf had not moved. Nothing now but the beating of his own heart, and the sense of an echo, gone as soon as apprehended. A delusion? Yet he could not escape the impression that he had been addressed. Encountered. That something had entered his consciousness. The experience left him as he tried to grasp it, like a dream flying, like dying embers that remember lightning. A thousandth fraction of a second it had taken, yet volumes might not be enough to say what it seemed to be. The most precious things in his life – Elizabeth's joy and Splodger chasing sticks and the gentle wisdom of Michael Aarons – all had gained (not lost, but gained) in value, because in some way they had to do with that. It left him close to weeping, yearning for a Paradise he had glimpsed but could not recall. It left him ready to shout and dance for delight in the promise of a destiny beyond conceiving. And following from it (though certainly not conditioning it) the summons – no, the challenge – to an act. Concrete. Measureable. Specific. Take the wolf to the Academy! That was what he was to do. And he was to do it now. He was no longer merely his own man. He served another. Turning his attention to the road, he slipped the car into gear.

Chapter Fourteen

The Devil Rides Out

To know that he must act was one thing. To do so, another. David was still not sure even in which direction the Academy lay. He drove slowly, trees on both sides of the road bowing and stirring in the wind. Another half-mile, and the pavement bore right, presenting to his gaze the mile-or-so distant sparkle of the Post Office tower, and, directly before him, a junction whose harsh, sodium glare contrasted strongly with the gentler lighting of the park. Something clicked in his memory. He turned the car left, and left again, confirmed in his decision by sudden signs pointing to St John's Wood and Hampstead. He drove more quickly. From behind him, Sabrina watched, and licked her paws, and sighed.

They had turned by St John's Wood church, and were passing Lords, when the enormity of what he was doing occurred to him for the first time. He pulled to the side of the road and stopped, waving past a following car. What on earth, he asked himself, was he up to? He was an officer of the law. A servant of the Crown. And here was an escaped animal, clearly valuable and potentially dangerous. His clear duty was to take it to the authorities. Who was he to be taking the law into his own hands? To be starting one-man crusades for justice because he thought he'd seen a vision? There was a word for that kind of behaviour, wasn't there? Megalomania. Wasn't that what they called it?

In sudden agitation he unsnapped the safety belt and got out of the car, slamming the door. Sabrina watched as he walked to the kerb and stood, breathing deeply. It was almost as if another self were arguing with him. A self he was not sure he wanted to hear. Leave aside then, said that self, the moment of vision (or delusion, if he preferred) – did he really think that everything else that had happened was merely coincidence? Was it coincidence that he was perhaps the one person in England who held in his hand threads that linked all of them – the Academy and Kakoyannis and Darrell and the wolf? That he alone had heard the questions that Brown was uncovering about the Academy's past, and Aarons' testimony about its present? Did he really think it was coincidence, indeed, that his own old friend should be the one who could give that testimony, and just when he needed it? And granted all that, could he still go on believing it was coincidence that the wolf that had escaped once should escape again (as she certainly appeared to have done) and that out of all the men and women in England who might have been on the right spot at the right time to find her, he should be the one? That she should seem, indeed, to have been looking for him? Did he really believe that it was all coincidence?

All right, he found himself responding. Something was going on, and he was part of it. But he was still a policeman. Never mind the jokes about PC Plod – there were procedures. And they were there for a purpose. A case was being built against the Academy. Not yet strong enough to bring to court, but the evidence was coming. The pieces were beginning to fit. Why then the hurry? What was so special about tonight? At the instant the question formed itself in his mind, the answer came. All Hallows Eve. The very last thing Michael had said to him. The witches' festival. Again the hair shifted on the back of his neck, and he shivered slightly. Superstitious nonsense? It was certainly coincidence. And there was that word again. Coincidence. Another coincidence? Or were there just too many coincidences? Would tomorrow really be too late?

With that, the real problem sprang to light. He didn't want to do it. It was like his reluctance to go and see Darrell. Only worse. This time the stakes were higher, and the risks immeasurably greater. What would happen if something went wrong? If he were stopped? He could just see himself trying to explain to his Superintendent. Or to a magistrate. Or to Elizabeth. (No, that wasn't fair, Elizabeth and Michael were about the only two people in the world to whom he could imagine explaining all this.) But the fact remained – he could be fired from the force. He could lose his pension. He could even (he suspected) go to gaol. And did he even know what would happen if he actually got the beast to the Academy? Well?

Nothing. Silence had fallen over the city – one of those curious lulls that sometimes affects the busiest place. Only the distant hum of traffic and a relentless moon. ('He is both manifest and concealed: manifest in order to uphold the whole: and concealed for He is found nowhere.') Damn. It seemed as if the universe were waiting to see how he, David Adam, would decide.

At 11.37, the attack came.

It is difficult to describe, since Elizabeth herself was at no point entirely clear what was happening. Only certain features can be identified. The first was emotional. As she sat at the dressing-table brushing her hair she was aware of enormous depression. A black, towering wave that filled her with nausea and threatened destruction. She, the house, the whole world – all were fat and helpless worms confronting an enormous and malignant carrion crow.

The second feature was to do with her senses. More precisely – to do with hearing. The roar of wind, fanned by a million wings. There flashed into her mind the fleeting memory of a plague of locusts, seen long ago on television. But this rose and fell in blasts of sound that pierced everything – the room, the furniture, her head – overwhelming and reducing her to chaos.

Which blended into the next feature. Her mind. Everything was muddle. She could focus on nothing. Dimly, she was aware of Splodger diving under the bed. She tried to stand, perhaps with a notion of using the bedside telephone. As she did so, she found herself wondering if David had paid the bill. With every atom of strength remaining, she struggled for control, and must have managed to cover the three or four feet to the bed, for she found herself kneeling beside it, fumbling at the instrument on the bedside table. For a moment, she actually grasped the receiver, but could not hold it. It fell from her hand and swung uselessly at the end of its cord.

Finally, heat. Stifling heat, that came with a stench of decay. The roaring mounted in intensity to a pitch of physical pain, and the impression of the locusts was now so strong, she could have sworn she saw huge mandibles and beating, monstrous wings. Being in an agony she called upon God, and heard no answer. Then she fainted.

Chapter Fifteen

The Coming of the Beast

The conflict was over. Right or wrong, he must do it. Or, alternatively, he could do it and he would. At that moment, a philosopher's attempt to oppose freedom and necessity would have seemed to David quite meaningless. He had recognized what was necessary for him, and in that recognition, he experienced freedom. He was fearful, and he was elated. He returned to the car.

Ten minutes later he drew up in a vacant space between parked cars, two doors away from the Academy for Philosophical Studies. Pulling on the brake, he switched off the engine, and looked back at Sabrina. Already, she was pawing to get out. She seemed to know exactly what to do. He first made sure that the street was deserted, then leant across and opened the door. He watched her slip through once more with that almost incredible grace, lope silently to the Academy's entrance, and disappear into the shadow of the porch. With her departure the car seemed emotionally as well as physically emptied. It was as if he had lost a friend. It was also as if he had pressed the switch that launched a bomb. He pulled the door close, and settled himself to wait.

Tom Wardle was sweating profusely. Of the long invocation that the Chairman had uttered, broken by occasional responses from Darrell and Ashliman, he had understood not one syllable. But the gestures had been obvious enough, and something in the very sound seemed to weigh upon him. Now they stood in silence. The vigil had begun. Stifling heat, alcohol, the just-completed ritual – all filled him with nausea. Only greed for power held him to the task, coupled with a certain dogged compulsion to finish what he had begun. Irma Ashliman and Reginald Danby had performed their parts like automata. Horror oppressed them too, though long schooling had brought them to a point where they experienced absence of feeling rather than distaste. Only James Darrell seemed to gain a positive pleasure. His work in many spheres had accustomed him to use the powers of life and death for his own ends, and in that to find satisfaction. So now, to reverse the great symbols of creation and eternity troubled him not at all. A faint smile played about his lips. He glanced sideways at the Chairman. At present he stood in awe of that figure. Yet the ceremony represented a boundary, even for the Chairman's powers. And the Chairman was old. What then when the boundary was crossed? What of the New Order? The Chairman's invitation to mastery was already, in Darrell's view, a sign of weakness. The old man needed support. He could no longer handle everything alone. What then of the future? The prospect was brilliant.

And what of the Chairman? Together with his acolytes he had sung a litany of praise and longing for the loss of all joy. Deeper than any of them, deeper than Nikos Kakoyannis, he knew what that loss meant. They sought power. He saw beyond power in itself, to the meaning of such power, and perceived it as idiocy; lonely and meaningless gibberish in a universe without hope. Death without end. And even so, he longed. The Chairman sought power, to destroy power. The entire New Order, in his hands, was to be a weapon of destruction, including at last the destruction of itself. For the Chairman judged the very act of creation, the divine fiat bringing light out of darkness, as evil beyond all evil, and the source of evil. His life's work was to fling back that act of creation in the Creator's teeth – the earth without form and void, and darkness upon the face of the deep. Where that could be restored, and the working of the Creator Spirit undone, there humanity passed judgment upon God, and the world was avenged. The Chairman alone knew the name of the Academy's master, whom the Hebrews called Ha-Abad-don and the Greeks Ho Apollyon: the Destroyer.

A lecturer, late leaving the Academy after closing drinks, opened the main door to the street, and was swept aside as if by the wind of God. Ten flights of stairs the wolf mounted in a whirlwind, to hear once more the call from the court of Solomon, the word of power. Sabrina obeyed, finding in that cry her summons to joy and high adventure. Straining her heart to the utmost, she crashed against the upper door – once, twice, till the slim, civilized lock burst, and she entered the temple in an ecstasy.

They had summoned the beast, and to them the beast came. Light streamed behind her as she leapt to the altar, suffusing her in gold as she scattered their relics. The Chairman knew instantly whose servant had come, and saw the divine parody, the glorious mockery, that transfigured the thing he had chosen. He knew, and he loathed. The others, questing power, saw hope ruined, and the terror of power turned against them. Only Tom Wardle, in the midst of his dread, was paradoxically conscious of a certain tremendous relief. The struggle was over. He yielded himself, almost with content, to what had come. To all of them it seemed that their ears were filled with the sound of fierce hail and many waters. Then came a rushing wind that billowed the hangings and shook the building. Lampstands crashed, dragging the curtains with them. Flames licked and reflected in spreading oil, shimmered in mounting heat. Leaving the worshippers, the wolf departed.

Chapter Sixteen

The Notebook

David was beginning to doze when Sabrina's scratching at the car door startled him into wakefulness. He opened it quickly, and the wolf crept in, tail down and paws bleeding. She was carrying something in her mouth – something she deposited gently on the front seat. Then she dragged herself to her place in the rear and lay there, broken. In a movement of compassion, he held out his hand and she licked it, surprisingly gentle. Their eyes met, his with concern, hers with animal trust, man and beast in their proper communion. Then Sabrina laid down her head, sighed once, and slept. She did not wake again. And for reasons he would not have found easy to explain, David was near to weeping.

He turned at last to the thing Sabrina had placed on the front seat. It was a black notebook, similar in appearance to the one Darrell had given him earlier. Inserted between its pages at several points were ribbons – apparently as markers. Opening at one of them, he was presented with what seemed to be more Hebrew. He grunted and gazed, straining his eyes in the yellow light, oddly fascinated by the curves and lines of the script. Dark and graceful it lay across the cheap paper. Serpentine. Ingratiating. Almost, he felt, if he looked long enough, he might grasp its meaning.

Shouts, crashes and the breaking of glass broke his reverie. He roused himself, snapped the notebook shut with something like distaste, and replaced it on the seat. He would leave the ribbons undisturbed, and handle the thing no further, at least until he had shown it to Michael. The sirens of an approaching fire-engine could be heard from the Bayswater Road. He turned the ignition.

It was hardly surprising that he did not notice a face that gazed malignantly down at his car from a third-floor window, and continued to gaze as he drove away.

He drove slowly back to St Andrew's. He needed above all to talk, and was relieved to find lights on in the church, and Aarons in the Lady Chapel, contemplating his young friends and the Academy and the Lord of Hosts, offering himself, in union with the divine Word, as channel and intercessor. David went in and sat beside him.

'Well?' said Aarons.

And David told him. Told him the story so far as he knew it. Of Nikos Kakoyannis and the cathedral. Of the wolf. Of Darrell. Of the sequence of deaths. And of what had happened now. Finally, he handed him the black notebook.

Aarons took and held it for a moment, then opened it and started to read. After a while, he turned to the places marked by ribbons and examined those. Then he returned to the main text. For ten minutes he read while David watched. As he read, his lips tightened and his hands began to tremble. Suddenly – it seemed the gesture cost him an effort – he slammed the book shut and flung it from him onto the wooden pew. There was a pause, whilst he collected himself. At last he spoke, in a whisper.

'Destroy it.'

'What?'

'Destroy it.'

'But –'

'We are in peril every moment it exists. If ever you trusted me in anything, do what I say. For God's sake destroy it – now!'

For David, such an appeal from Aarons could brook no denial.

'The fire in your study?'

'Yes. We can relight it if necessary.'

They went back to Aarons' study, the priest leading the way with nervous impatience. There they were able without difficulty to rouse the embers into life. David knelt in the hearth and tore page after page from the notebook, consigning each to the flames, until all were consumed. He threw in the ribbons, and watched them twist and char. Finally he stirred the coals with a poker, making sure that not one legible shred remained. Then he looked at Aarons, who seemed to relax.

'Well? Is that good enough?'

'It is good enough. Let me explain.'

David sat himself in an armchair and waited.

'If ever we had any doubts about the evil of the Academy,' said Aarons, 'I think we can set them at rest. By what guidance the wolf brought you that book, I do not know. But it held the key. *Beriyt et-Mavet* – "*A Covenant with Death*".' He hesitated, and then went on. 'It spoke of a tradition that hitherto I have only heard whispered. A tradition as old as Solomon.'

Again he paused, looked at the fire, and sighed. 'There is a ritual. We will not speak of its details. Even its syllables are a kind of corruption. According to our tradition, Solomon the king tried to use it for a good end, but even in him it was vanity, and a cause of evil. Once, years ago, in Vienna, I was shown a fragment of it. Even that was held to be a most powerful talisman for evil. Any who would perform that ritual with serious intent would destroy the earth for their whim. And the notebook contained it – I think, complete.'

'And the Academy? They were going to do it?'

'I think so. You saw the ribbons?'

'Yes.'

'Like a missal. Certain passages. Certain invocations – prescribed for certain days. Those marked by the ribbons were all for All Hallows Eve. It was about to be used. Perhaps was being used. I am almost sure.'

'And you believe that such a ceremony could really achieve something? Something evil?'

'You say you met one of these men. Darrell. James Darrell. Tell me – did he seem to you a man who would waste his time on children's games?'

'No, he didn't.'

Aarons nodded. 'And this was no game. Oh, of course – if your question means, can God be mocked with impunity? – the answer, in the end, is No. But what is the instrument of his providence in this? Maybe even you!'

'Oh.'

With all that Aarons said, David retained a certain sense of disappointment that the evidence had been destroyed. 'But surely, it wouldn't have been dangerous if you'd kept it?'

Aarons shook his head. 'Especially dangerous for me. For I could have used it.'

'But you wouldn't.'

'David – am I not telling you? I felt power in the very form of its words. It was all I could do to throw it down. Believe me, I could not swear to have had that book in the house for one day, and not succumbed. With you it was safer – at least for a while – for you could not use it.'

'Oh,' said David, 'Well. It's good to know there's some virtue in stupidity.'

'There is no virtue in stupidity,' said Aarons sharply, 'and you are not stupid. There is virtue in innocence. God be thanked you have a measure of it. Maybe that is why the book came to you. I don't know. But remember – even you it would have attacked in the end. Even you. You are not *that* innocent.'

Suddenly David remembered the fascination that it had exercised over him during his brief, unwitting handling of it in the car. He shuddered. 'Yes,' he said. 'I see what you mean.'

After a while, they went to the car and Aarons looked at the body of Sabrina. He fetched a spade and together they buried the wolf without mark in the garden that adjoins the vicarage and church, standing for a moment by the grave, whilst the priest commended her to whatever destiny should be proper for a beast in the good providence of God. They returned to the house.

Chapter Seventeen

The Journey

Darrell had left his colleagues as soon as the trouble began. He was a man who never, if he could manage it, allowed himself to be without a way of retreat. As soon as Sabrina entered the temple he perceived the situation, stepped smartly aside, and walked quickly behind the hangings to a door that led to the back stairs. The door was locked but he had a key. He used it swiftly and stepped out. On the landing he closed the door behind him and locked it again. It would not, after all, do to have the monster following him.

He paused to consider. Then, since shrieks and crashes from the temple still sounded uncomfortably close, he descended a couple of floors and made his way to the Board Room. Here the noise was dulled and he could think more clearly. For his colleagues, he gave not a damn. He doubted very much whether any of them would survive. He had a vague recollection of seeing Irma Ashliman making for the far door, and it was possible she had got out by that. Danby had slipped and fallen in a pool of oil, and he recalled that Wardle had stumbled on top of him. He could not remember observing the Chairman at all. But it did not matter. None of them mattered. What mattered was that, regarding his own position, he was both angry and anxious. Angry because the Ceremony of Power had been interrupted and the precious notebook almost certainly lost; angry because the inauguration of the New Order was now indefinitely delayed; and anxious because interruption of the Ceremony must mean that his attack on Elizabeth Adam had been interrupted too. After only (as he calculated) about twelve minutes. Would twelve minutes have been sufficient? He doubted it. She was young, healthy (so far as he knew) and not lacking in either spiritual or mental resources (that, indeed, was what made her such an admirable offering). She was almost bound to have survived. And if she were not yet dead, or at least dead by sunrise, the offering would be incomplete.

He stood by the window, looking down on the street, and considered what his next step should be. As he did so, his attention was caught by a dark, slowly moving form that limped along the pavement. It was the wolf. Darrell peered, and to his utter astonishment saw clearly in the yellow light the face of David Adam as he let the beast into the car.

James Darrell was now truly shaken, and truly angry. So that was what the Chief Inspector was up to in London! But how. . . ? He could not explain it.

Darrell was shaken, but by no means beaten. He watched as David drove off, and then considered his own car, behind which David had parked. He looked at his watch. It was the woman, after all, who was the immediate concern, and there was still plenty of time. He could be in Salisbury in little over a couple of hours. Once there, revenge and expediency pointed in the same direction. Before sunrise, he must kill Elizabeth Adam.

David sat himself again in Aarons' study. He still did not feel tired, but he was worried. Deeply though he respected Aarons' opinions, and however much those opinions appeared to coincide with his own feelings, he remained uncomfortably aware, as a policeman, how little real evidence there was to give grounds for the wild action he had taken. He did not even know what destruction the wolf had caused, though it was obvious she had caused some. It was all very depressing. He sat back, made himself breathe more slowly, and tried to relax.

Next to the brass fire irons in the hearth there was something white. He bent forward. It was a small, roughly-torn triangle of paper.

'Is this yours?' he asked, as Aarons came into the study with mugs of coffee, 'or is it part of that book?'

He handed it to his friend. Aarons glanced at it casually, then looked more closely, his brow furrowed.

'This isn't mine. Where was it?'

'Near the grate. I just picked it up.'

'Then it must have fallen. David, my friend,' Aarons spoke with increasing urgency, 'would you do me a great favour and telephone Elizabeth?'

'What – you mean now? Is something wrong?'

'This paper. There is something here that I don't understand. But I don't like it.'

He passed it back to David who saw this:

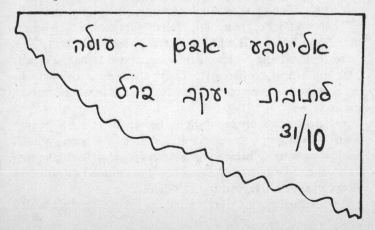

with certain other symbols.

'What is it?' he asked.

'It says – roughly – "Elizabeth Adam, the whole burnt offering of James Darrell" and, as you see, there – the date. Today's date. I don't know what it means, but I don't like it.'

David had taken the point, and was already dialling his home number. A pause. He held the instrument in the air so that both men could hear the engaged signal.

'At two o'clock in the morning? I'll try again.'

Still engaged.

His face taut with anxiety, David dialled the operator. The pause whilst she had the line checked was maddening, as were the cool tones in which she eventually informed the caller that this line appeared to be out of order, and she would have the engineers look into it.

David's fingers stabbed fiercely at the dial as he rang the number of the Salisbury police. 'Bill? oh – thank God. Look – it's David Adam. Bill – maybe it's nothing, but I can't get through to Elizabeth on the phone. And I'm a bit worried. Is there anyone near who could just check that she's all right?'

A pause. Then a response that Aarons could not hear.

'That would be great. You've got this number, haven't you? Good. OK – I'll wait for you to phone back then.'

He replaced the receiver and looked at Aarons. 'There's a car quite near, apparently. They're getting it to look in, and they'll phone me back. They reckon it'll be about fifteen minutes.'

It was actually only ten minutes before the telephone rang again. David leapt to answer it. 'Yes. Yes – here. What? Look, I'm coming back to Salisbury. Yes, it should take me – oh – a couple of hours. What? No, of course I'm not . . . I'll go straight there. All right. Thanks.'

He put back the receiver. 'Michael, I don't like this at all.

Two of our chaps went to the house. They've just radioed. There are lights on upstairs, but they can't raise Elizabeth. And something's on fire. They're going to break in. And they've sent for the fire brigade.'

Aarons' own look of anxiety deepened. 'I'm afraid this looks rather serious.'

'I know. Michael – I'm sorry – but I want to be there. I'm going to throw my things into a case, and go. I must.'

'Of course you must,' said the priest. 'However, I do have a suggestion.'

'What's that?'

'That I should come with you.'

'Would you?' exclaimed David. He could think of no one whose company he would rather have had at that moment. Then conscience assailed him. 'But look – I've caused quite enough trouble for one night already. Aren't you exhausted?'

'Don't be patronizing!' retorted the priest. 'As it happens, you are the one who has been rushing about all night, not I! Now – you get your case – and whilst you do that, there are a couple of things I must do.'

It took David only a few minutes to get his things together, but by the time he returned to the study, Aarons was replacing the telephone receiver.

'I think,' he said, 'that Norrie was a little surprised to be telephoned at this hour – but, like the good fellow he is, he'll cover the celebration for me. Now,' (he picked up his diary) 'tomorrow actually seems to be rather a good day for rushing off! Just a couple of notes for Jim, I think. If you would get your car started and out onto the road, by the time you've closed the gates, I believe I can be with you.'

'Right'.

Faithful to his word, the priest, overcoated and carrying a small brief-case, appeared through the side door seconds after David had closed the main gates. Seat belts were fas-

tened, the driving mirror checked, and they set off into the
night.

Ahead of him, Darrell could see the lights of Salisbury, and
was even able to make out the red light that sits on top of
the cathedral spire. He had stopped once for petrol at the
Fleet Service Station; apart from that, his journey had been
without incident.

Flames were still pouring from the upper windows of the
Academy and several fire appliances were assembled. A small
crowd had gathered to watch. In the general confusion, it
was hardly surprising that no one noticed a half-charred
remnant of humanity, pulsating with malignancy, that crept
out of a back door and began to drag itself from shadow to
shadow in the direction of East London.

At this time of night the roads were deserted, and David
drove well. In little over twenty minutes, he had reached the
motorway. The last time he had driven this way at night, he
recalled, Elizabeth had been with him. They had been to a
meal with friends in London. It had been one of those perfect
occasions when everyone seems wittier, more beautiful, and
more compassionate than usual. Then on the way back, just
as they came to the motorway, Elizabeth had become anxious, wondering if she had forgotten to leave the animals
their water. Suddenly as he remembered, David found himself passionately, agonizingly aware how precious she was to
him. Her concern for small people and small things. Her
utter honesty. She was a princess. A true princess. And if
that swine Darrell. . .
  'Steady, my friend.' Aarons' word recalled him to the
present none too soon. He was clutching the steering wheel
as if it were Darrell's neck, and the speedometer was hov-
ering between ninety and a hundred. The Basingstoke sign

flashed into sight, and he deliberately relaxed, easing the throttle back to a gentler seventy.

'Sorry,' he said, 'I was thinking about something else.'

'I know,' said Aarons.

Immediately after radioing the station, Sergeant Stillwell returned to the front door of the Adams' house. He could hear his colleague round at the side, still stamping on the embers they had found smouldering.

He rang the doorbell one last time and rattled the letter box fiercely. Then he stood back, making his decision about the best way to break in. At that moment, the glass panels on the door filled with yellow light. A few seconds later, it opened and Elizabeth Adam appeared, tousle-haired, a little confused, and looking (to tell the truth) remarkably pretty, Pooh fawning at her feet on one side and Splodger jumping about on the other.

Chapter Eighteen

The Assassin

For a while, even after consciousness returned, Elizabeth had lain still, unable to make out why the light was on, why she was on the floor, or what the noise was. Then came the memory of her extraordinary experience, mercifully softened by two hours of unconsciousness. Ugh! How horrible! What on earth had come over her? She shook her head in relief that she now felt more or less normal and got to her feet, albeit a little unsteadily. The telephone receiver was dangling from its cord and her hair brush was on the floor by the dressing table. Almost automatically, she bent to replace them, when Sergeant Stillwell made his final attempt on the front door.

'All right!' she called, 'I'm coming!' – then realized that whoever it was could not possibly hear. She went out to the landing and switched on more lights. Pooh appeared from behind a door and Splodger (sheepishly) from the top of the stairs.

'Sorry to be disturbing you,' said Sergeant Stillwell when she opened the front door, 'but we were a little worried, you see.'

'Yes. Of course. I'm sorry. I – I think I must have fainted.'

'And there's something burning at the side of the house. I dunno what it is. If you feel up to it, maybe you'd better come and look. It's made a bit of a mess of your garden, I'm afraid.'

As soon as Darrell turned into the road where the Adams lived, he saw the flashing lights of the patrol car. Warned, he pulled to the side under some trees. He could not see the house which stood back from the road and was fronted by more trees and a high hedge, but through the branches and foliage he thought he saw lights at about the level of the second storey. After a few minutes the fire service arrived. This did not surprise him, for the attack was meant to be marked by fire. The question was – how much damage had the fire done? And what had happened to the woman? For the moment, he determined to watch and wait. There was still plenty of time.

Stockbridge always reminded David of a wild west town in a film. He was not sure why. Perhaps because the houses were built right on to the road. Obviously, it had rained here earlier. The roads were gleaming, and for the last half-mile he had been obliged to reduce speed. There was no point in reaching Salisbury in an ambulance. Even so, he was driving quickly by most standards as he swept in fine spray up the High Street and changed down for the hill and the steep, sharp bend that mark the approach on the Salisbury side. Aarons watched the road, and said nothing.

To say that the fire had made 'a bit of a mess' of the Adams' garden was understatement. On that side of the house (it was the side nearest London, though no one noticed) the Adams were flanked by a high stone wall. From the wall to their home was an area about eight by eight yards. And the whole of that area was shrivelled, blackened, and withered – like a giant sheet of paper to which someone had held a match. A wheelbarrow and a wooden frame had still been burning when the police arrived. The wall of the house itself was scorched and frames of the lower windows charred and smouldering. It was this that led the police to summon the fire service, fearing that the wall might be on fire inside. And whilst they waited, they did what they could to stamp out embers and suppress the flames they could see. Fortunately, the effects of earlier rain had prevented the fire spreading.

The fire brigade arrived, and Splodger, recovered from her previous fright, barked furiously. The firemen calmed Splodger, but were as much at a loss as anyone to explain the fire. The flames seemed to have no origin. It was, the senior officer said, as if the ground itself had overheated. They checked the wall thoroughly (in the process making an indescribable mess of the study), but found nothing. That part of the fabric, as it happened, did not even contain wiring. They dug the garden, and two inches below the burnt surface found themselves dealing with normal Wiltshire earth. It was utterly baffling.

Elizabeth, in the midst of this, was actually beginning to enjoy herself. Sergeant Stillwell had told her of David's telephone call, and that he was now coming home, and (though she hoped to goodness he would drive carefully) it really was rather pleasant to think of her own knight errant rushing through the country to protect her. The attack itself was beginning to seem more and more like a bad dream, best forgotten. And for the present, if she had to have the house full of large men in helmets at two o'clock in the morning, she might as well enjoy it. So she offered coffee, and biscuits and cake, all of which the large men (it being a quiet night) were happy to accept. Splodger too moved sociably among the guests, accepting a biscuit here and a piece of cake there. Only Pooh retired huffily to the bathroom.

BEWARE OF ONCOMING BUSES
IN MIDDLE OF ROAD

The familiar sign loomed into the glare of David's lights, half a mile from the outskirts of the city proper, and he reduced speed. In years of motoring, he reflected, he'd never met an oncoming bus yet, but no doubt there had to be a first time for everything. The low bridge passed, he opened the throttle again. Only much later did he recall that it was too late for the buses to be running anyway.

For over an hour Darrell waited with carefully controlled impatience whilst the firemen checked and double-checked, fetched equipment from their vehicles and returned for more equipment. At first he entertained some hope that Elizabeth might be dead. But as time passed that hope faded. At last the firemen left. Their manner was cheerful, even slightly raucous. A while later the police also returned to their car, and they, he was sure, turned at the gate to bid someone 'Good-night'. The woman was alive.

Well, that need not matter. There was time enough. He waited a little longer, then unlocked the glove compartment and took from it a revolver. This, he reflected, was excellent – the Smith and Wesson .38 was actually a police weapon. It had been stolen for him, months before, by his police contact, more as a test of ability and willingness than for any special purpose. Now, to use it for this particular task was ironically satisfying. He checked the safety-catch, slipped the gun into his coat, and made sure that the road was clear; then left the car and walked quickly towards the Adams' gate. He stopped. Perhaps the police had left someone behind? He shrugged, and went on. If there were others there, he had the gun and he had surprise. Probably he would kill them too. He could not go back now.

At last they had all gone – including two splendid firemen (one a Londoner) who made her laugh until she wept, and a bashful constable who obviously admired her. Elizabeth went back to the kitchen, which was tidier than she might have hoped. Two of them had actually washed up, and though they had hung tea towels in the wrong place, and left the sink greasy (typical men!) at least they had tried. That was on the credit side. Against it, the state of the study was now impossible to describe. Apart from anything else, it would have to be redecorated. But that, she decided firmly, could be thought of tomorrow. For the present, she would make more coffee, read a book, and wait for David. Absent-mindedly, she let Splodger out of the side door and filled the kettle.

Darrell opened the Adams' gate quietly and slipped through. It was his second surreptitious visit to the house within hours and he knew the terrain. There were now no lights visible from the front, save those that obviously lit landings. He moved to the left, and immediately was aware of a glow from ground floor windows at the side of the house. Further progress found him crouched behind bushes, facing the lighted windows. They looked directly into the kitchen, which was empty. Several minutes passed. Then Elizabeth appeared in the doorway and went to the cooker.

Darrell stood up. He had the window, the kitchen, and the woman in plain view. The familiar smile played about his lips. He raised the gun, and prepared to fire.

At that moment, several things happened almost simultaneously. The first was that the figure of a man leapt with a shout into Darrell's line of sight, obscuring his view of the window and Elizabeth. For a fraction of a second, Darrell hesitated out of mere surprise. Then, having already decided what he would do if the police had left someone behind, was about to fire anyway when –

The second thing happened: which was that an infuriated Splodger, goaded beyond enduring by the presence of yet another intruder in her garden, hurtled round the corner of the house and angrily assailed Darrell's right trouser leg. At the same time, the figure between Darrell and the window lurched and disappeared with a crash of foliage and a shout in what sounded like German.

The third thing was that in the diversion thus created, David Adam was able to approach Darrell from behind and, in precisely the manner approved by the Wiltshire Police Academy, attacked, overpowered and disarmed him, whilst Splodger barked angry encouragement.

'David – are you all right?' Aarons approached somewhat breathlessly. It was he, of course, who had flung himself into the path of Darrell's intended shot and then, less heroically tripped over a root.

'Yes – fine – thanks.' David's voice was also breathless. 'This,' he added as if by way of introduction, 'is Doctor James Darrell.'

Summoned by the noise, Elizabeth appeared from the side of the house.

'Good grief,' she said, 'I thought Splodger had found a hedgehog.'

Chapter Nineteen

Michael Aarons Explains

From the time when Elizabeth, at David's request, went to telephone the police, the entire wait probably took no more than eleven minutes. Yet it was, for Michael Aarons, eleven minutes of agonizing length. Darrell sat on the couch and stared into space, refusing to meet their eyes, refusing to communicate, the contemptuous smile still upon his lips. Normally, Aarons would have felt it appropriate to leave a man in such a position to his own thoughts – allowing him opportunity to come with dignity to an acceptance of defeat. But this was different, for there grew in Aarons' heart a certainty that for this man time was almost over: that if he did not reach out his hand now, there would be no other chance. He spoke once, and was ignored. Then, with a bluntness born of desperation – 'I know what will happen at daylight.'

Slowly, Darrell raised his head and looked at him. 'So?'

'So – you know what I am talking about?'

'I know what you are talking about.'

'Then – there is help for it. Even now – there is another way.'

'You think I'll ask your help whilst your fan stands there watching how clever you are?'

'David – I'm sure you would leave us for a moment?'

'It's of no consequence,' Darrell interrupted him. 'That oaf can stay or go, for all I care. You can bring in the whore too, if you want her. I will never, never ask for help from you. Or any like you. You ask too much.'

The words were more biting because they were said without emotion. Aarons saw David's jaw tighten and felt a surge of anger in himself. But this was no time for the indulgence of personal feeling.

'I ask for nothing,' he replied.

'On the contrary,' said Darrell, 'you ask for everything.' And turned away.

Michael Aarons bowed his head and was silent. For he knew that what Darrell said was in one sense true, and he had no answer. Never had he been more conscious of personal inadequacy. Never more hotly aware of the limitations of his own compassion.

As they took Darrell to the waiting car, Aarons' plucked at David's arm and beckoned him aside.

'Tell them to watch him carefully until morning,' he said. 'I think he will try to kill himself.'

'To kill himself? Why?'

'Too complicated to explain now. Just say – oh – I think he's the type. Anything. But get them to watch him. I'm serious.'

'All right. If you say so. It can't do any harm.'

A few minutes later, David came back from the patrol car. Elizabeth and Michael were sitting in the kitchen.

'All right,' said David, 'I told them to watch him. They'll see he can't damage himself. Now – what's it about?'

'Let's take it in order,' said Aarons. 'First – Elizabeth – have you ever seen anything like this?' He produced the triangle of paper that David had found in the hearth. Elizabeth looked at it, and started with surprise.

'Why, yes. Something very similar. I found it this morning. Here – I'll get it.'

She returned from the hall a few minutes later, bringing the triangle that she had taken from the front door that morning. She gave it to Aarons, who laid the longer sides of the two triangles together. They fitted perfectly, and formed a roughly-torn square.

'What on earth?'

'I can explain in a minute,' said Aarons. 'First, tell me about what happened here earlier. Before the police came. You say you fainted?'

Elizabeth told them the story of her ordeal as well as she could remember it.

'Right,' said Aarons. 'Now – at what time do you think this happened?'

'Well – I don't know exactly. I went to run the bath at about eleven, I suppose. And then – oh – I remember. I put my watch down on the dressing-table when I went into the bedroom, and it said half-past eleven. I noticed.'

'And that's when it happened?'

'Well, no. I brushed my hair for a bit. Five minutes. I don't know.'

'And then it happened?'

'Yes.'

'Say – between 11.35 and 11.45?'

'I should think so.'

'All right. Now – David. Do you know when you reached the Academy?'

'Not to the minute. It was eleven when I left the vicarage – I noticed the church clock. The traffic was reasonable so, say, twenty minutes to Regent's Park. I guess I was about five minutes there – though I'm not sure. Ten minutes to Lords? Then I stopped again – maybe another five minutes. Then I drove to Bayswater. I remember thinking how lucky I was being with the lights on that bit. That's, say, another ten minutes? What's that? Fifty minutes for the whole trip. That feels about right. Ten to twelve then.'

'And you released the wolf at once?'

'Yes.'

'And it entered the building.'

'Yes.'

'And that's all you saw until it returned with the book?'

'Yes.'

'Then,' said Aarons, 'I think I can see the timetable. You, my dear,' he turned to Elizabeth, 'were under an attack. An attack instigated by Darrell. This divided paper is an ancient form. The curser takes one part. The other he passes to the cursed. In this case – you. And some kind of ritual would inaugurate the attack. Now, something unusual and destructive happened here between 11.35 and 11.45. We know that, not only because of what you felt, Elizabeth, (which could be put down to imagination) but also because of the fire, which certainly was not imagined. A fire whose origin no one can yet explain. Whatever was happening here seems to have lasted long enough to have had some effect – but then it stopped. Why? Well, we also know that the wolf entered the Academy at about 11.50 and caused some kind of disturbance. She returned from the disturbance with a notebook, and the notebook contained a ritual. It also contained half of the curse. We must assume that, for by no other means could the curse have come to my study. So, whatever was disturbed by the wolf had something to do with the curse. And that, I suggest to you, is why the attack ended before it achieved its intention. What you and the wolf did, David, was to stop a ritual that was aimed at killing your wife. If you had not taken the wolf to the Academy, it seems to me that Elizabeth would now be dead – in the charred ruins of this house.'

'But if they could do all that, why should Darrell have come after me with a gun?'

'Because the ritual was stopped – and because your death

was necessary to him. Tonight. To someone, or something, he had promised it.'

There was silence.

'What's this to do with him committing suicide?' asked David.

'The man has failed. Elizabeth still lives. I fear that in such affairs, if the offerer fails to keep his bargain, he must pay the penalty himself.'

'That's what you were talking about to him? And why you think he'll try to kill himself?'

'That's right. And he knew what I was saying. Actually, it makes no difference whether you watch him or not. You can call it auto-suggestion, if you will. Call it what you like. But if I'm right, that man will be dead by morning.

4.37 a.m. PC Jenners drove slowly from the direction of Commerical Road in London's East End. Ahead of him, the decaying splendours of the Town Hall, the Nautical School, and the East India Dock Road. It had been (comparatively) a quiet night. Not long to go now. His eye was caught by something moving slowly on the opposite pavement. Squat, awkward, with a strange limp. 'What the hell's that?' he asked himself. A huge articulated lorry roared out of no-where, heading for Aldgate. Momentarily, his view was blocked. When the lorry had gone, there was nothing. Was he seeing things? Or had it (he? she?) turned off? Jenners pulled right into Newell Street and stopped. Nothing. He got out. Still nothing. Except a faint, charred, decaying smell. As if Friday's dinner had gone bad before it was cooked. He peered up and down again. The drains round here must be awful. He shrugged, and got back into the car. A few minutes later, he was proceeding down the East India Dock Road. The episode did not even seem worth reporting.

Chapter Twenty

All Saints' Day

6.50 a.m. The police, to do them justice, did all that could reasonably be asked – even before David Adam (as a result of what Aarons said) telephoned them again, and emphasized the need for care. Darrell's cell and his person were checked. Nothing visible that could be used for self-destruction was left accessible to him. That was standard procedure. In addition, someone looked in on him every fifteen minutes throughout the night. But it would have made no difference if they had stayed with him. Only a specialist could have spotted the instrument that Darrell always carried, and perhaps no one could have stopped him using it when he chose.

Now he stood beside the narrow bed and looked up at the small barred window. As yet it showed no sign of light, but he knew that it could not be long.

Aarons was perfectly correct. Darrell had offered a life and a life was forfeit – his or that other's. And since the other still lived, it must be his. He knew the rules. He was under no illusion that his continued existence was of the slightest importance to the power he had served, or that the purposes of that power would be halted by his death. Even now, however, he would retain what control he could. He would not wait for the sun. He stood, facing the barred window, and for the last time a faint smile played about his lips.

In the few seconds of life remaining after his teeth had crushed the tiny cyanide capsule, there came to James Darrell the amazing possibility of another kind of bargain and another kind of universe. Beneath the still eyes of heaven, he responded to that possibility. And in the light of his response, he died.

Officers, checking his cell a few minutes later, found the body.

6.50 a.m. Total blackness. But the Chairman was already blind. An instinct that needed no light had dragged him seven agonizing miles across London, avoiding people and prying eyes, leading him through mean streets and dark alleys, barren sites and builders' rubble, past wire fences and careless watchmen, until at last he had plunged into shadow and come to this place. Here, eighteen centuries before, iron-hard legionaries had invoked the Light-Bringer, consecrating their strength and courage to the service of justice and truth. Centuries later, fools calling upon a power they did not know had vowed the altar to Darkness. A virgin had died. Evil men had fought and cursed. And fire had gutted the buildings above. Then for years the chamber lay silent, hidden and forgotten, waiting.

Now the Chairman had come, contrary to his plans, against his hope. The New Order, the way of destruction over which he would preside – all was lost. His company was broken, himself dying. He knew well enough what the fire had done to his flesh, and the little time that even his fanatic will could sustain its failing energies. A way remained. He would invoke the Destroyer alone, as had Kakoyannis before him. Yet not as Kakoyannis. He had no illusions. In this place, prepared for so long, what he was about to do would be like a lighted candle to escaping gas. Undoubtedly he would perish. It did not matter. Hell's yearning is to become incarnate. Its frustration – that the flesh is holy. But where there was willing offering, there the power of destruction could, like a cancer, find something to grasp; and, like a cancer, destroying what it grasped, would spread. That would be, for the Chairman, satisfaction enough.

Even could he have seen, he needed no book. So many times he had pored over the rite since Darrell brought it to him, its rhythms and words were part of him. He had neither chalice nor wine. Neither circle nor lights. Neither symbol nor protection. Desire alone must suffice.

His body screamed in protest, but the will pierced and silenced it, concentrating all on the last preparation. The mind cleared. The agony itself was caught up and used. A focussed energy, refusing every distraction of joy or love, directing all to its utter resentment. Still some vestiges of expression floated to the surface. Still the sullenness fought to be verbalized. 'It was their fault. . . It was his fault. . . I never had a chance. . . It isn't right. . .' Even that, he denied. The very remembrance of words was a tribute to meaning. And meaning also must be rejected. To be perfect, his resentment must be wordless, mindless and directed everywhere: approaching the Satanic perfection of which Milton spoke – 'that fix'd sense of injur'd merit'.

He raised his hand, swayed, and might have fallen; but the altar stayed him. At the very moment when James Darrell died, the Chairman, in scarcely a whisper, began the rite.

1.10 p.m. Michael Aarons ate a light lunch with Elizabeth. David was back on duty. The news of Darrell's death weighed no less heavily on any of them because Aarons had guessed it would happen. In addition, Elizabeth, who had borne the events of the night with remarkable calmness, was now feeling her own reactions.

It was, as she reflected afterwards, rather odd. She might

have imagined she would feel fear. Or anger with her attacker. Or supernatural dread at the strange form of the first attack. (To her surprise, the distinction between that and the attack with a gun did not actually seem very important. They were, after all, only different kinds of weapon – one crude, the other less crude.) Instead, as she told Aarons, what actually affected her so far was a sense of outrage. Not particularly against Darrell. Rather, against a universe where people like Darrell could do the things they did. Where her own simple right to existence could be threatened because some one else decided he wanted her out of the way. She felt angry, violated and hurt.

The two of them were glad of each others' company, but it was not a cheerful meal.

2.10 p.m. Waving aside offers of a lift, Aarons ambled to the railway station. Despite all that had happened, it was good to be in the delicate, wintry sunshine. His own feelings about the affair were by no means unmixed. He shared David and Elizabeth's distress, certainly. He was appalled by what had happened to Elizabeth. And it would be long before he forgot the face of James Darrell. On the other hand, it seemed possible that last night he himself had actually saved Elizabeth's life. David, indeed, had assured him of this several times. And although he did not feel any particular pride in the matter, he could not be unaware of a sense of relief that at least he had not failed again.

It had been, all in all, an amazing few minutes, beginning as they sped into the road where the Adams lived. David, who in some ways was really a remarkably good policeman, had spotted Darrell's car. Twice previously he had seen it – once in Darrell's drive, and once, without realizing it at the time, when he parked behind it outside the Academy. It was enough. Something clicked in his memory. 'Darrell's here!' he muttered, and leapt out. Aarons followed, and by mere chance (or providence), chose a way that brought him sight of the intruder first. At the very instant when he saw the gun raised, and guessed what was about to happen, he remembered Steiner. The ancient fear threatened to hold him back; and it was, in a way, as much for Steiner as for Elizabeth that, despite fear, he hurled himself forward. As he recalled, he seemed almost to stand outside himself, using a force that was not his own to overwhelm his reluctance and drive him into the path of Darrell's bullet. Somehow, somewhere, he hoped (and believed) that Steiner knew. It was, after all, a vindication. One man's death, twenty-eight years earlier in a camp in central Europe, had not been for nothing. Even his own treachery had been taken up and used. Through them, Elizabeth Adam now lived. It was as if, for a moment, he had been allowed to glimpse a pattern. And how very fitting, he noted, that with that accomplished, he should not have been left in any position of heroic dignity or death, but that his own life should have been spared (it appeared) by the action of that ridiculous and beautiful little dog, and a ludicrous sprawl put an end to any pretensions he might have had to be a man of action!

The train to London did not appear to be in much of a hurry; but then, neither was he. He settled himself in a corner with a book he did not expect to read and watched the fields. What, he wondered, of James Darrell? Poor fellow. How explain a man like that? It seemed to Aarons that, in God's providence, he owed even Darrell a debt, however little Darrell might have intended it. In what state of mind, Aarons wondered, had he died? Remorse? Repentance? Fear? He could only guess. And perhaps even guessing was a kind of impertinence. 'No one is ever told another's story. Each is told his own story.' Wasn't that what Aslan always said in the Narnia books? Something like that.

That evening, Michael Aarons preached at St Dunstan's, Stepney, and received the holy communion. As he did so, he prayed for David and Elizabeth; for James Darrell; and, with a tranquillity that was wholly new to him, he prayed for Josef Steiner, his friend.

Chapter Twenty-one

Afterwards

February. The Players Number Six and the Embassy Tipped were as strong as ever. And Irma Ashliman had a headache. She got to her feet, nodded to the speaker, and slipped through the door. Piggy-eyes was off duty, but Bill Maclaren was in his usual place.

'Good evening, Bill.'

'Hello, Mrs Parker. Nice to see you. You haven't been with us for a long time.'

'No,' she hesitated – then relaxed slightly. 'The fact is, we've had a couple of rather serious set-backs. In the organization. They've kept me rather busy.'

'Sorry to hear that. Nothing you can't cope with, I hope.'

She smiled. 'Oh, no. Nothing we can't cope with.'

'That's the ticket, Mrs Parker. Don't let 'em get you down.'

She smiled again. 'Thank you, Bill. I won't. Good-night.'

'Good-night.'

She was nearly out of the door – then, 'And don't stay away so long next time!' he said.

She laughed, and looked back at him. 'All right,' she said. 'I won't!'

On the way to the car, it suddenly occurred to her that Bill Maclaren found her attractive. A few paces further on, and it came to her that she felt in exactly the same way about him. When he had said, what was it? – 'Don't stay away so long next time!' she had felt a quite girlish pleasure. Such was her surprise at this discovery, she stopped. Then she frowned. In the world she had chosen there was simply no place for that sort of thing. None at all. She walked slowly on. On the night of the fire at the Academy she had been badly frightened. Since then, she had once or twice caught herself indulging in bouts of irrationality such as this. She really must keep a tighter grip.

A few minutes later the Lotus was speeding in the direction of Steadman Street.

March. Splodger saw a rabbit. In hot pursuit she rushed through ferns and long grass, leaping and yelping with delight. David followed more slowly, gazing thoughtfully at the sunflecked hillside. He paused to admire a group of celandines, then straightened abruptly and turned up his collar against a stiffening breeze. The day had been warm but with the approach of evening it was freshening.

Soon, he knew, he must talk to Michael Aarons. The resolution was forming. What would come of it, he couldn't imagine – but he must talk, long and seriously. Four months – a third of a year – had passed since the affair at the Academy, since the death of James Darrell. And David Adam had changed. Not changed dramatically, so that there were raised eyebrows or problems about work. But subtly, in a thousand small ways that he knew and Elizabeth sensed. Work itself, once a consuming interest, was something he continued to do well, but without his former heart. He felt himself to be one who gets on with a job in hand whilst waiting for something to happen. He knew, too, that he was gentler with Elizabeth, and in many ways more sensitive than before; but there was also a distance between them. He was fighting a battle and even she, for the present, was not part of it. They had tried to talk of it several times but without success, only ending with his plea to her – be patient. And now, of course, she too had changed. They had learnt that this very day.

There she was, seated on a grassy mound, waiting for him. Wind ruffled her hair and she was shading her eyes from the declining sun.

'Aren't you getting cold?' he shouted.

'No – yes – I suppose I am a bit.'

'Come on then, we'd better go. We can't have you taking risks – not now you're in a "delicate condition"!'

She laughed and got to her feet. Splodger scampered on. Hand in hand they walked back down the narrow path that leads to the city.

Appendix

Extract from article 'Asmodæus' in J. Hastings (ed.) *A Dictionary of the Bible*, Edinburgh, T. and T. Clarke, 1898, Vol I, pp. 172–173.

'Asmodæus ('ŠMDY Tobit 3:8, 17) is probably identical with the evil demon of the ancient Persian religion, Aeshma daeva . . . When the Hebrews borrowed the name, they connected it with ŠMD, to destroy. Hence this is the being called *ho holethreuōn* in Wisdom 18:25, and 'BDWN = *ho apolluōn* in Revelation 9:11. In the latter passage he is styled "angel of the abyss" and "king" of the destructive creatures shaped like locusts, but with men's faces and with flowing hair. The only mention of Asmodæus in the Greek Bible is in Tobit, where he is described as *to ponēron daimonion*; Vulgate, daemonium neqissimum; but in the Aramaic and Hebrew versions "King of the Shedhim". . . The Shedhim are the *daimonia* of the gospel narrative . . .'

Extract from the *Babylonian Talmud*, Gittin, 6a-c.

'Why did the King require the demons? For the reason suggested in this verse: "When the house was built, it was with stone prepared at the quarry; and neither hammer nor axe nor any tool of iron was heard in the temple while it was being built." Solomon said to the rabbis, "How shall I manage unless I use tools of iron?" They answered, "There is the *shamir* that Moses brought for cutting and shaping the stones of the Ephod." The King asked them, "Where can it be found?". . . They said to him, "We do not know; but it is possible that Ashmedai, the Prince of the Demons knows." Solomon said to them, "And where is he?" They replied, 'He is in a certain mountain." Upon this, Solomon despatched to that place Benaiahu ben Jehoiada, bestowing upon him a chain on which was engraved the NAME, and a ring upon which was also engraved the NAME. . . . So Benaiahu went down and cast the chain over Ashmedai and made it fast. When the demon awoke, he began to struggle, upon which Benaiahu cried, "The Name of your Master is upon you! The Name of your Master is upon you!"

'As Benaiahu was leading him, the demon came to a palm tree and brushed against it, and it fell. He came to a house and smashed it down.

'When they arrived at Jerusalem, Ashmedai was not brought before Solomon for three days . . . After three days he went in to see him. He took a reed and measured out four cubits, and cast it down before the King. "Look," he said, "when you die you will own no more than four cubits in this world. But for the present you have mastered the entire world – and yet you will not be content until you have mastered me also."

'Solomon answered, "I desire nothing from you. My desire is to build the Temple, and I have need of the *shamir* . . ."

'Solomon kept Ashmedai with him, until he had built the Temple. On one occasion, when he was alone with him, he said, "Wherein are you greater than we are?"

'Ashmedai said to the King, "Remove the chain from me, and bestow upon me your ring, and I shall show you."

'So Solomon removed the chain from him, and bestowed upon him the ring. Then the demon swallowed him, and placing one wing on the earth, and another on the sky, he threw him four hundred parasangs. In reference to that, Solomon said, "What does man gain by all the toil at which he toils under the sun?". . .

'Solomon went about begging, and wherever he came, he said, "I the proclaimer have been king over Israel in Jerusalem." When he came to the Sanhedrin, the rabbis said, "See here – a lunatic does not stick consistently to one thing. What does this mean?" So they asked Benaiahu, "Does the king send for you?" Benaiahu answered, "No." The rabbis then sent word to the queens, asking, "Does the king come in to you?" The queens sent back a message, "Yes, he does." The rabbis then sent to them to say, "Examine his leg!" (for the legs of a demon resemble those of a cock – see Tract. Ber 6a). The queens then sent back to say, "He comes in stockings, and he comes in to us in the time of our separation, and he also sends for Bathsheba, his mother."

'The rabbis then called for Solomon. They gave him the chain and the ring on which was engraved the NAME. When Solomon went in to the royal house, Ashmedai flew away at the very sight of him. Yet the king remained afraid of Ashmedai, and so it is written – "Behold, it is the litter of Solomon! About it are sixty mighty men of the mighty men of Israel, all girt with swords and expert in war, each with his sword at his thigh, against alarms by night." '

Extract from the *Revelation to John*, 9:7–11.

'In appearance the locusts were like horses arrayed for battle; on their heads were what looked like crowns of gold; their faces were like human faces, their hair like women's hair, and their teeth like lions' teeth; they had scales like iron breastplates, and the noise of their wings was like the noise of many chariots with horses rushing into battle. They have tails like scorpions, and stings, and their power of hurting men for five months lies in their tails. They have as king over them the angel of the bottomless pit; his name in Hebrew is Abaddon, and in Greek he is called Apollyon (or Destroyer).'

The Fantasy Stories of George MacDonald

The Golden Key
The Gray Wolf
The Wise Women
The Light Princess

The complete short stories of the originator of modern fantasy literature.

Lilith

George MacDonald

A haunting exploration of good and evil.

Phantastes

George MacDonald

The dream-like novel which had a formative influence on C. S. Lewis.